MURDER BECOMES ELECTRA

A LOVE STORY

By the same author

FICTION

Tourist Attraction

The Experiment

The Exterminator

Freddy Hill

The Surrogate

Secter Ingredients

Best Summer Job

Jazz Jazz Jazz

Bliss Incorporated

Freddy Hill in Las Vegas

The Catalogue

Harrassment

NON-FICTION

The Right End of the Stick

The Joy of Freeloading

Better than Working

FOR CHILDREN

The Chocolate Touch

John Midas in the Dreamtime

The Orphan and the Billionaire

Eskimo Surprise

John Midas and the Radio Touch

John Midas and the Vampires

John Midas and the Rock Star

A Trunkful of Tricks

Chocolate Magic

The Best Game in the World

MURDER BECOMES ELECTRA

A LOVE STORY

PATRICK SKENE CATLING

Somerville Press

Somerville Press Ltd,
Dromore, Bantry,
Co. Cork, Ireland

First published 2017

Designed by Maurice Sweeney
www.mpsbookdesign.com
Typeset in Adobe Garamond Pro

ISBN: 978 0 9955239 82

Printed and bound in the EU.

for Diana

1

Annapolis, Maryland. A beautiful morning this Spring, ideal for love. It was the day his nine-year-old daughter would get him a pack of strawberry-flavored condoms.

Southern zephyrs were wafting aphrodisiac salt air up from Chesapeake Bay, across Spa Creek. There was an aroma of fish from the Market. Between the dome of the State House and the masts of sailboats and cabin cruisers at the City Dock, honey-colored early sunshine was warming blossoms of dogwood, magnolias and azaleas and the faded-rose eighteenth-century brick facades of a National Heritage street of small, precious row houses.

In front of a particularly desirable bijou residence, the sun was smiling on a painted cast-iron African-American midget jockey in scarlet and azure silks, an Italian white marble urn of crocuses, a pair of polished brass carriage lamps, a fanlight, a black door with a bronze squirrel's-head knocker, and a closed-circuit surveillance camera. The owner was a security-conscious romantic.

This was the home of Arnold Bosworth, the 34-year-old creator of Squidgy the Squirrel. People who encountered Mr Bosworth for the first time at local social gatherings never would have realized, until they heard his name, that he was a writer of stories for young children. He seemed so quietly confident, they presumed he must be someone important, perhaps in industry, commerce, or government. It is only a short commute from Annapolis to Washington.

He was tall, trim, neatly barbered and conservatively tailored in the fashion of a gentleman in an English TV drama series about life above stairs. Furthermore, he had the clear, steady eyes that distinguish some of the most beguiling, $20 million-a-picture, young Hollywood actors. In a police file (heaven forbid!) he would be described thus: Height—5' 11"; Weight—168 lbs; Hair—light brown; Eyes—blue; Complexion—fair.

Only a writer for children? Ah, but Squidgy the Squirrel had been a big bestseller in hardback and paperback for several years and was on countless primary-school reading lists. Arnold had been encouraged until recently to foresee the time in the near future when Squidgy would be in talking books, TV cartoons and a syndicated newspaper comic strip. Soon, Arnold had been led to believe, there might be Squidgy dolls, Squidgy T-shirts and Squidgy baseball caps. He understood that negotiations were imminent to begin manufacturing Squidgy Cola and Squidgy chocolate bars. The books had widely disseminated the Squidgy philosophy, which was founded on good old-fashioned family values, and enabled Arnold to support his own little family in enviable comfort.

Up the Bosworths' softly carpeted stairs, at the end of the short passage to the back of the house, the master bedroom was opulently furnished, for the most part in pink and gold, around a queen-sized bed. On that beautiful, amorous morning, nothing was happening in the room, but there was talk. The first voice was a high warble as pure and pretty as the music of a flute.

"Do you love me? Do you?"

Arnold, lying not very comfortably on his back, half-opened his eyes and saw her anxious, voracious frown. He smiled.

"Good morning, sweetie-pie. Of course I do. You know I do."

"Well, say it."

He sighed. Why did she feel insecure? She was insatiably demanding. He was complimented, but even so....

"I loved you yesterday," he said. "I love you today. I'll love you tomorrow. OK?"

"I love you too."

"Good."

Standing beside the bed, she leaned down close, and hugged his neck.

"Ouch!" he protested with a spluttering attempt to laugh. Angelica was surprisingly strong for a girl of nine. She was also deliciously feminine. Sugar and spice and all that's nice—that was the traditional recipe, wasn't it? Alice-in-Wonderland hair, a peachy complexion, eyes bluer than the summer skies. She was a cuddly girl with dimples, but the determined urgency of her desire made her seem destined for early status as a femme fatale.

From the far side of the double bed, there was an impatient groan.

"For heaven's sake, get that kid out of here. It's only a few minutes after seven."

"It's a school day," he reminded his wife. He tried joviality: "Time for all of us to rise and shine."

"I don't like having Angelica in the room before I'm dressed."

"Oh, really, Cindy darling!"

"Yes, oh really. She stares at me."

"It's admiration. Your Mommy's a very lovely lady. Isn't she, Angie?"

"She's not my Mommy."

Angelica's mother, Arnold's first wife, was dead, having fallen head-first from the balcony of a hotel's penthouse suite. Cynthia had been Angelica's step-mother for nearly two years. One of those fine-featured, rather flat-chested ectomorphs with auburn hair, hazel eyes and pale skin who usually wear so well when carefully maintained, she had been a playful, childless divorcée when Arnold and she had met.

Now, almost 36, she was an increasingly reluctant surrogate

"Mom." The word made her squirm.

"Oh, knock it off, you two," she said. "Why don't you take her to school today, Arnold? You know how I hate Mondays. I'd like to start the week gradually."

"All right. All right, darling," he said. His early-morning erection, unused, was already history. His early-morning erections these days were almost always unused. He and she really should have a talk. In the meantime, he might as well get out of bed.

"Kindly go away, Angelica, dear," Cynthia requested, emphasizing "dear" with teeth clenched.

"Please, Cindy. Please, Angie," he beseeched them. He found that the middle was a lousy place to be in.

But Angelica had already left the bedroom. A beautiful day had turned into just another ordinary one. Arnold was quite glad about yesterday's message on the Ansa-Fone. His publisher sometimes sent messages, even on Sundays. She wanted him to go up to New York for a "one-on-one strategic-planning *tête-à-tête.*" A one-day break, he thought, would do him good.

2

Cynthia stayed in bed, listening to news of traffic flow, frontal systems and peace-keeping military interventions, while consoling her clitoris. Arnold and Angelica, dressed for the day in brotherly-sisterly T-shirts, jeans and trainers, were having breakfast in the kitchen.

The externals of the Bosworth house were immaculately preserved, as befitted its place of honor on Cornhill Street, close to the center of the city's National Historic Landmark District. Inside the antique building, however, modern functionalism discreetly prevailed. As the Annapolis & Anne Arundel County Conference & Visitors Bureau proudly proclaimed, "The District reflects

Colonial beginnings, federal vitality, nineteenth-century vivacity and contemporary vision." Angelica sat at a farmhouse-style pine table and thought her secret thoughts. Arnold stood at a stainless-steel counter and operated gadgets that hummed and buzzed and screamed, processing blueberry muffins, oranges and coffee beans.

The camaraderie of the kitchen, he liked to think, made their breakfast "a meaningful bonding experience." She gazed adoringly at his straight back in white cotton and blue denim and wished and wished that he and she could be together, alone, always.

"Waffles?" he asked, holding up the plug of the waffle iron.

Angelica smiled and shook her head. She thought it was kind of cute that he believed she might still crave syrup. Her smile tilted wistfully, acknowledging he had not yet noticed her new maturity.

"Syrup's full of calories," she admonished him.

"Excuse *me*."

"A glass of milk, please. Skimmed milk."

Bobo, Angelica's best friend, and she were on a diet. They had been on it for three days, having agreed that puppy fat sucks.

"Anything interesting at school today?" Arnold wondered, taking a stool at the table with his steaming Squidgy mug.

"For Computer Science, we're visiting a Research and Development facility, out in the County someplace. This morning we have Sex Education." Like Citizenship and Music Appreciation, Sex was a snap course, an easy A, a super way to start the week.

Sex! Arnold looked away from his young daughter, up at the clock on the wall.

"Well, finish your milk," he said. "We'd better get the show on the road."

Passing the foot of the stairs, he shouted goodbye. There was no response.

Because the weather was fine and the distance short, they

walked—up Cornhill, around State Circle, along School Street, around Church Circle. Above the brick tower of St Anne's Church, the clock on the grey steeple said 8.10. Arnold and Angelica had been inside the church yesterday, standing side by side singing "Rock of ages, cleft for me/ Let me hide myself in Thee…." The church was packed with its smart WASP congregation. Cynthia, who had announced Sunday-morning fatigue after the rigors of Saturday-night hospitality for six dinner guests, was not among those at their communal devotions.

Father and daughter walked on in the brightening sunshine, toward the low-lying white concrete and green-tinted glass of John Paul Jones Elementary School. He and she said nothing for a while. Arnold broke the silence.

"What's on your mind, angel-child?" he asked. He had an inexhaustible supply of pet names for her.

"Nothing."

"Aw, come on. Nobody ever thinks nothing. Is anything wrong?"

"Who do you love most?"

"Whom. What do you mean?"

"Out of Cynthia and I?"

"Cynthia and me. Object of the preposition."

"Who do you love most?" she persisted.

"That's an impossible question. I love you both, in different ways. Father-and-daughter love and husband-and-wife love are different."

"Because you fuck Cynthia?"

For a moment he was speechless. He stared down at her, his eyebrows raised in shock.

"Angie! Where did you get that word?"

She looked up at him in mild surprise.

"The kids at school say it all the time. People in movies, on TV.

Cynthia sometimes says it when she's mad. Once I heard her say it to you when she wasn't mad."

"It's not a polite word, Angie. I wish you wouldn't use it."

"I wish a lot of things. I wish she didn't live with us. I wish it was only you and me."

"You and I."

"You and I."

"Grown-ups," he explained in the patient, tolerant manner of enlightened parenthood, "grown-ups who love each other, like to live together. Mommy has passed on. Life must continue."

"But that Cynthia! What's so great about her?"

"You're being unfair, sugarplum. You really should try to get to know her better."

"I hate her. She hates me and I hate her."

"Of course she doesn't. You're imagining things."

"I am not. She said she hates me."

"I find that very hard to believe," he said, though after more drinks than usual she sometimes blurted out very hurtful remarks. "Look, Angie, here's school. We'll have to discuss all this some other time—all three of us. I can't understand—"

He was interrupted.

"Hi, Angie!" yelled Bobo, a tall, skinny 10-year-old brunette, who, like Annapolis as advertised, was vivacious and vital. She had a loud voice.

"Hi, Bobo!" yelled Angelica, immediately changing into schoolgirl mode. The two girls met at the school gates at the beginning of every school day as if being reunited after a long separation.

"All right, lambkin, I'll leave you here," Arnold said, lowering his face for a goodbye kiss. But without another word, Angelica ran off. As he watched her go, he felt his unkissed cheek with questioning fingertips.

3

Angelica was going through a phase, Arnold told himself. There had been a previous prickly phase, when her mother was alive, but Angelica had been sweet to him at the funeral, comfortingly holding his hand and giving it a reassuring, affectionate little squeeze as Beatrice's coffin was lowered into her grave. Angelica had been much braver, more philosophical, about her mother's tragic fall than he had.

He shook his head, as if to clear it of gloomy memories. It was time to complete his exercise, walking the long way home. He must teach Angelica to accept her stepmother, he resolved, to respect her at least; possibly, some day, to love her. He strolled along sunny College Avenue, past the miniature campus of St John's College, which had once adopted the convenient notion that all life could be understood by reading The Hundred Great Books. Angie read a lot. That was a start.

There is nothing like education, he reflected. Information, knowledge, wisdom. In rare consensus, politicians all proclaimed it is every citizen's right to he provided with the educational know-how to pursue happiness—and to catch up with it. And what, he asked himself, makes a person really one hundred per cent happy? Right! An enlightened, glitch-free sex life.

It is hard to believe today but as recently as the middle of the twentieth century few couples used to live together unless they were married. Many young women were not sexually tested until their wedding night. Lagging far behind the world's most primitive tribes, in which nubile maidens were ceremonially initiated into womanly ways, most mothers of the so-called developed countries used to offer their daughters only mutually embarrassing, rudimentary briefings on the eve of marriage. Some mothers, too awkward to provide even perfunctory guidance, being themselves, quite likely, not so hot in bed, merely recommended a how-to-do-it manual, such as Goodspeed's *So You Want to Have a Baby*. Marriage was a sexual bingo game, and there were many losing cards.

Since those days of mystery and imagination, sexologists, with increasing authority, have pointed out that sex education should begin at the primary-school level. Like before-need funeral arrangements, which take a lot of the hassle out of bereavement when the time comes, before-need sex education was established in order to minimize the boo-boos of adulthood. There is no such help as too soon.

Freud rightly observed that human sexual awareness begins in infancy. According to him, babies of both genders fall in love first with their mothers. There are males who persist in this emotional attachment much longer than is good for them. Females, on the other hand, quick to notice they have no penis, often soon transfer their devotion to their fathers, and maintain that orientation even into puberty and beyond. Oedipus Complex, Electra Complex. Oedipus has always got the bigger share of the publicity, but Electra was just as passionately mixed up.

Adolescence is far too advanced for the beginning of sex education, as the large number of teenage pregnancies and abortions shows. These days, changes are being made. Young children are invited to maternity hospitals to check out the miracle of birth. Father and child, with their arms around each other, sit close to Mommy and watch her deliver. The sight is enough to make children careful.

Angelica was still an only child. She and Cynthia had never been brought together in the communion of the delivery room. However, thanks to a well-funded, progressive school system, Angelica was already well on her way along the Information

Superhighway. She knew all about the biology and mechanics of sexual intercourse.

Arnold's morning exercise, less than aerobic, proceeded in its habitual leisurely, thoughtful fashion down King George Street. Which King George did the street memorialize? Not the crazy one, surely? The street ran parallel with the boundary of the extensive grounds of the United States Naval Academy. In this republic, in which Church and State are separate, in accordance with the Constitution, State Circle is more imposing than nearby Church Circle. And though civilian government supposedly controls the military establishment, the Naval Academy dwarfs its civilian academic neighbor.

He wondered whether the future of Annapolis and Angelica would be culturally secure. Would the world remain safe for children's books? He hoped that not too many of the forty-five hundred midshipmen were cheating in their exams this year. He liked to feel that most of the officers in charge of the aircraft carriers and nuclear submarines of the most powerful nation in the world have a reasonably clear notion of what they are doing. After all, naval officers, like parents, teachers, librarians and publishers, are only human. The midshipmen, hedging their bets, give lip-service to God and the statue of Tecumseh, an Indian (native American) chief, that is ritually propitiated before all important athletic contests and the graduation ball. On certain special weekends, opportunities are given for the exercise of heterosexuality. Would Angelica one day become a Navy wife? His little Angie.

As usual, Arnold was relieved of such somber considerations when he turned right on Randall Street, and right again, heading for home and his study, where Squidgy the Squirrel, waiting in the memory of the computer, represented childhood innocence and idealism.

4

After his walk, it was time for another cup of caffeine to get his working day properly started. When he went to the kitchen, Cynthia was there. She was relaxing in an aura of soap and Joy, in the chair in which Angie had been sitting. The nine-year-old's rival was fresh from the shower and her dressing-table mirrors. Cynthia's turquoise silk robe enhanced the auburn of her hair, the hazel of her eyes, the Day-Glo red of her lips.

Her breakfast, like his, consisted most importantly of coffee. The orange juice and muffin were incidental. Arnold and his wife had recently got into the habit of taking sleeping capsules at bedtime. She called them "Barbie dolls," which made them seem innocuous. She took hers with hot chocolate in the bedroom. He took his with brandy in the electronic entertainment center they called "the library." The drink and two green and pink capsules enabled him to drift into oblivion like an embryo floating in blood-temperature amniotic fluid. It was possible to sleep, he discovered, without a preliminary orgasm. There was no risk of insomnia; barbiturates could be depended on. Cynthia's physician, when scribbling her first prescription, had said that the soporifics were useful for establishing a pattern of regular sleep. After they did so, Cynthia would be able to give them up. But she was not in a hurry; nor was Arnold. They eased frustration. Having been chemically brought down in the evenings, however, they both needed artificial help in the mornings to get up to something like scratch. So far, strong, black coffee had proved sufficient to do the trick.

"You look wonderful," he said. He meant it; she did. Holding his mug aside, he leaned forward to kiss her. She ducked and twisted out of reach.

"I've just done my face," she pointed out.

"Yes. It's gorgeous." He sighed, leaned back, and sipped more coffee.

"Are you working today?" she wanted to know. "Don't forget: dinner tonight with the Ersdales. Jeanette says one of your special fans is going to be there."

"Oh," he said in a voice of ineffable melancholy. Then he somewhat brightened. "Don't fix anything for Wednesday. I have to go up to New York to see Naomi." Naomi Swartkop was one of New York's most dynamic, hands-on editors of books for children. Her name was a by-word in The American Association for Literature for Young People, a body of formidable power and decisive influence. "You know what that means," he added with what was intended to be an ingratiating smile. "I'll be beat by the time I get home."

"A slave to your art," Cynthia commented, her eyes aglitter with sarcasm.

"Her decisions are vital. To both of us—to all three of us."

"I know. Oh, brother, don't I know it! I want a new car. Everybody's driving BMWs. They're becoming very, very boring. And there's Martha's Vineyard to think of."

He was well aware of Martha's Vineyard. A summer house in the Vineyard was Cynthia's latest concept of a must-have. And it had to be there. Other venues were nowhere.

Arnold gulped the lukewarm, sooty dregs of his coffee.

"Time for the torture chamber," he said, rather feebly, for the daily joke had worn thin. He entered his study and gratefully shut the door. His study was the one part of the house where his life seemed to be his own. The room was about the size of an average prison cell, but it was as immense as the imaginary universe he shared with millions of children between the ages of seven and eleven, his "target readership" as Naomi called them. In his study, hidden from the rest of the household, he could escape to the farthest reaches of space and time. It was here, after he had been made providentially redundant as a writer of television commercials, that he had begotten Squidgy. And it was here, through the magic screen of his computer, like Alice's looking glass, that Squidgy and he had travelled together to fantastic realms of rewarding adventure.

The success of the resulting books had provided his antique Chinese writing table of dark-red lacquered wood, the indigo and umber Afghan rug on the oak parquet floor, the black-leather armchair in the corner between the two walls of floor-to-ceiling bookshelves filled with first editions of his own book, bound in crimson morocco, and other works of children's literature. Success had provided Arnold with his costly house and almost everything in it, including his costly wife.

In his recent heyday, he had gained a standard of living, a lifestyle, which required industrious support. Squidgy stories, so easy to read, were being invented more and more laboriously. Arnold had exhausted the obvious, conventional magical formulas—Squidgy's achievement of magic invisibility, Squidgy's magic ability to fly, Squidgy's magic changes of size, from tiny to gigantic, Squidgy's magic journeys into the past and future, Squidgy's discovery of a magic lamp with its omnipotent Arabian genie.

Arnold told himself he was not suffering from terminal writer's block; but he felt bound to admit to himself that he was experiencing a distressingly prolonged period of writer's hesitation. Several months had elapsed since he had dispatched his last typescript by express courier to New York. Naomi had not responded with the usual ecstatic e-mail, followed by a magnum of Bollinger. After a long delay, there had been only an uncharacteristically formal, brief snail-mail letter, dictated by her personal assistant to a secretary, without any of Naomi's encouraging e-mail intimacy. He was willing to concede, in the course of a soul-searching 4 a.m internal monologue, that there was a certain weakness in concluding Squidgy's Caribbean fantasy with the words "It was only a dream." Fantasies have to seem real. Perhaps there was a problem, but there was no need for Naomi to be shitty about it, no need to depersonalize her way of communicating. Perhaps they were overdue for one of their lunches.

Anyway, he told himself, some children were still loyal to Squidgy. Their letters continued to arrive, though in noticeably diminishing numbers. Whenever he felt uneasy about his prospects for the next fiscal year, he turned to the letters for reassurance.

He took the top letter from the small pile of correspondence awaiting his attention. E.B. White, after the publication of his masterpiece, *Charlotte's Web*, was inundated by so much fan mail that he sent only a printed form-letter in reply to children's praise. But Arnold tried to follow the example of the erstwhile most prosperous children's writer of all. Right to the end, Roald Dahl answered every letter individually. He even took the trouble to flirt with teachers, whose approval could so beneficially affect sales. "We never say 'Dear Miss Thingy,'" he wrote. "We put, 'Lovely, gorgeous Sheila and all the clever children in your class.'"

Arnold smiled gratefully at the pink envelope in his hand. The flap was decorated with an inscription scrawled in letters of red: "I LOVE SQUIDGY"—with a red heart, of course, in place of the word *love*. There was another promising sign: there was a small circle, instead of a dot, over the I of SQUIDGY. A circle over a capital I was a bonus. The fan was evidently a girl of delightful girlishness.

> "Deer Arnold Bosworth," he read, "I am in the Third Grade of Bismarck Elementary. My name is Lisette

> Kanopoulos. Im ate yers old. I have chestnut hare and brown eyes and my hobies are skoober diving and naycher study."

Lisette's handwriting was above average for a third-grader of the twenty-first century. Her spelling, perhaps derived from text messages sent and received on her mobile, was average.

> "I hav an ole sister," she confided. "She is cawled Carmen. I hav a Golden Labrador Retreever cawled Missy. She has glassis and braysiz on her teeth wich I dont. My teecher is cawled Ms Whipsnade. She has assined me a projeck wich I got to rite to my favrit awther so heer goze. Wen did you decide to be a riter. How did you get the ideer for Squidgy. How long duz it take to rite a bok. Do you have a famly. Do you have a dog. Wot kined. Wot are yor hobies. Pleez send a big foto of you sined by you with a red felttip pleez. Well I mus go now.
>
> Yaw NUMBER WUN FAN
> sined LIZETTE KANDOPOULOS
> rite bak soon."

Sometimes Arnold felt that E. B. White, not Roald Dahl, had the right idea. The questions were always the same. Why not always send the same answers? On further consideration, why bother?

Arnold carefully tore the letter in halves and quarters and dropped them into his wastebasket. His wayst baskit.

5

Meanwhile, at John Paul Jones Elementary School, Dr Nancy Schick, PhD, whose dissertation had thoroughly prepared her for "The Linguistics of Cross-Cultural Constructivism," was trying to persuade her twenty-six fourth-graders to settle down and sit quietly at their desks. Generations of affluence and high-protein diet had produced acerbic children inclined energetically to raise hell, in the friendliest, most cheerful way.

The Education Department of Digby College, in Digby, Ohio, had been strong in the philosophy of elementary education in hypothetical terms. Ms Schick (she did not insist on being addressed as Dr Schick) had not been prepared practically for the fact that television had reduced the American attention span at all ages to the duration of programming between two segments of commercials. But even for the sophisticated children of Anne Arundel County there was a subject still able to arouse their curiosity and keep it aroused for the best part of an hour at a time.

"Time for sex!" Ms Schick winsomely announced. The word was still potent. The boys and girls sat motionless and silent, except for an exchange of giggles between two girls in the back.

"Bobo! Angelica" Ms Schick called. "Please pay attention. You won't be allowed to sit together if you disturb the others with your silly whispering. Today's lesson will be of great significance to all of you, boys and girls, especially girls. We are going to learn about contraceptives—how not to have a baby unless you want to." She wrote the word *contraceptives* in white chalk on the blackboard, slowly and accurately, as it was such an important word. "Not many years from now," she said, facing the class again, "this will concern you personally."

The median age of the children in Angelica's Class was her own age. But there were a few girls who had been held back a year or more, because of illness or too many failing grades. The school's regular policy was to push children through, willy-nilly, in the hope that in their freshman year in college they would be taught to read and write, sufficiently grammatically to get by in their future professions, trades and private interpersonal relationships. However, there were special cases that required pre-collegiate attention. There was one girl in Ms Schick's class, for instance, an amiable simpleton of twelve, whose only distinctive achievement was that she had already started to menstruate. She was the sort of girl, physically precocious and mentally dim, who attracts adolescent boys, and for whom, therefore, instruction in the use of contraceptives was timely, possibly urgent.

In teaching about sex, as about other subjects, the teachers of J.P.J. used visual aids whenever they could, since research indicated that written words alone were often imperfectly understood and quickly forgotten. Today Ms Schick unlocked the cupboard beside the blackboard and produced a visual aid that was most reliably memorable. The realistic, full-size, pink plastic model of human male genitalia was always a big hit with fourth-graders. By repeatedly squeezing the scrotal sac, it was possible to inflate the penis, to achieve erection; and, by inserting a neat little plastic plug in the base of the penile shaft, it was possible to sustain the erection as long as required. In this capability, the model was superior to a real live organ.

When Ms Schick had procured the model, through an internet catalogue (www.maritalaids.com), she had taken it, in her briefcase, to her lonely apartment for close observation. She still sometimes took it there overnight. Now she placed the model on her desk at the front of the classroom, so that everyone could see. With the deft efficiency of practice, she rapidly pumped the penis up to its optimum height. Inflated till hard and shiny, it measured almost seven inches from its root to the tip of its corona. As she contrived this elevation, as wonderful as Jack's beanstalk, she managed to maintain an expression of objectivity, in the tradition of her vocation.

Bobo nudged Angelica in the ribs.

"Quit it!" Angelica hissed, without deflecting her gaze from the phenomenon on the desk. Ms Schick, on previous Monday mornings, had shown the class movies in the educational documentary series "The Facts of Life." Angelica had seen moving pictures of flaccid penises at rest and penises rampant in action, in all the configurations that athletic young men and women were able to demonstrate. But movies are only movies. Here was reality in three dimensions.

"Weird!" Bobo marvelled. "How would you like one of those stuck up inside you?"

"Cut it out!" Angelica angrily muttered. Bobo was distracting her from a fascinating day-dream.

Ms Schick introduced the model penis with a brief propaganda harangue. In early middle age, she was already both overweight and withering. Fat was turning into limp crepe. Her large breasts sagged as if partially deflated. Hormonal decline was causing the growth of fine down on her jowls, and an almost invisible mustache. As a teacher on the public payroll, she was obliged to tell her pupils all they needed to know about sex. As an independent, single person, she was not about to recommend progenitive sex, and no authority could compel her to do so.

"Our planet," she began, her piggish little nose wrinkled by disdain, "is dirty and diseased. The worst disease, by far, is human. There are too many people in the world. They multiply like maggots in rotten meat. Millions more are born every day. They poison the earth, the water and the air we breathe."

"Here she goes again," Bobo whispered. "Ms Schick's famous green sermon. Violin music, please."

"The easiest way to avoid having babies," Ms Schick went on, speaking with sudden evangelical zeal, "is simply to refrain from sexual intercourse. Many people, however, find they are unable to refrain. Fortunately, for these weak characters, scientists have devised methods against conception. Some women rely on contraceptive pills, which are effective unless they forget their daily dose. But the surest contraceptive is—"

"A pair of scissors?" Bobo suggested.

Angelica pinched Bobo's arm. Bobo pinched back. A scuffle ensued.

"All right, Angelica!" Ms Schick exclaimed. "That's enough. Come up to the front and stand by my desk. Instead of disturbing the class, you can do something useful. As I was saying," she said, as Angelica went forward, "the surest contraceptive is the condom. After lunch, we are going to visit the R. and D. facility of the Adonis Corporation's splendid new factory, where we will see condoms being manufactured and tested by state-of-the-art automation. But first we are going to see how easily condoms are applied. I'm going to ask Angelica to demonstrate the procedure. It's fool-proof."

Ms Schick opened a tiny silver envelope and extracted a rolled-up condom of powdery white latex, which she held up and brandished, like a conjurer claiming that the next trick would be above board.

"Now, Angelica. Place the condom on top of the penis—no, the other way. That's it. With finger and thumb, grasp the ring of rubber and unroll it slowly downward. Good, until it covers the full length of the penis. There! The condom's small teat at the end is designed to prevent breakage and spillage that would permit all those wriggly, microscopic tadpoles, the spermatozoa, to swim up to the ovum, the egg. Very well. Thank you, Angelica. You may return to your place. The rest of you will approach my desk, one at a time, to examine the penis close up, protected for safe intercourse, safe from AIDS and safe from unwanted fertilization. All right Timmy. You first."

When Angelica got back to her desk, Bobo grinned at her and

said: "You should see your face. It looks like your cheeks are on fire. Were you very embarrassed?"

"Of course not. I was thinking about Daddy."

6

Ms Schick led her fourth-graders from the yellow school bus to the main entrance of the factory, a model of modern light-industrial design, a low, flat-roofed, white building very much like their school, as hygienic-and expensive-looking as anything in Silicon Valley. Think of all the eager customers, the billions of Asians, Africans and Latin Americans out there, and the millions of regular Americans here, not to mention the Australians, Inuits and the gallimaufry of Europeans, most of them with access to television several hours a day. The media are busy inflaming billions of libidos, and the medical industry is busy supplying billions of condoms.

The public relations director of the Adonis Corporation was a pert young lady, as neat and lively as a well-groomed, well fed Pekinese. Heather Pinkney's brunette hair was tidily bobbed and her make-up minimalist; her grey and white seersucker suit fitted well and the heels of her dark-grey shoes were of moderate height. She was the sort of true believer who could have gone far in Scientology or Tupperware, but her aspiration was even loftier. Her eyes lit up when she talked condoms.

Ms Pinkney was standing in the middle of the white-marble foyer, waiting to greet the visitors. Their arrival and her orthodontically correct smile were precisely on schedule.

"Ms Schick!" she rhapsodized. Nothing gave this dedicated PR lady more pleasure than giving her spiel on the wonders of Adonis condoms. "Boys and girls! Welcome! Please follow me."

The teacher and children sat in the front three rows of an auditorium like a small, luxurious cinema, and their beaming hostess took her place behind a pulpit at one side of the platform. After her long introduction, which was part sermon, part statistical sales pitch, the lights dimmed, and curtains parted to reveal a screen.

The film perfectly complemented the morning lesson about overpopulation and infectious bodily fluids. A voice-over, as warm and sincere as a TV news presenter's, described the hazards of sex without condoms (including premature ejaculation), while documentary footage showed a modestly rumpled Bob Geldof with starving children in Ethiopia and Elizabeth Taylor socializing with skeletal men in a hospice in San Francisco.

"But life can be beautiful," the commentator assured the audience, as the camera zoomed into a palatial bedroom, where a beautiful, high-protein, undiseased couple demonstrated The Product. "With the inspiration of Venus, and the protection of Adonis," the mellifluous voice concluded, "the honeymoon never ends."

The music synthesizer was silenced, the curtains closed, and the lights came up. The fourth-graders were thoughtfully silent. The prospect of a healthy, active puberty promised so much.

In a vestibule, Ms Pinkney distributed surgical masks in preparation for a tour of the factory proper.

"Prophylaxis is the key word," she pointed out. She conducted the masked children, like a group of midget surgeons and nurses, into a controlled atmosphere in which computers and android machines hummed and clicked twenty-four hours a day, in the endeavor to satisfy global demand. She recited production figures with hushed reverence and called attention to the rigorous means of quality control, by electronic testing and random human inspection.

The children were beginning to whisper and fidget. This part of the visit was beginning to bore even Ms Schick, who kept glancing, less and less furtively, at her watch. Their attention span was close to term. She was as relieved as her class when Ms Pinkney brightly announced it was time for reflection and refreshment.

In keeping with the high standards of the whole Adonis operation, there was a fancy cafeteria. Tinted picture windows overlooked a terrace with flowers, a lawn, a fountain and an awesome, bigger-than-life statue of Adonis, just like the statues of Greek antiquity, except that this replica of the classical figure sported an immense erection clad in a marble condom. Reproduced in many sizes as the corporation logo, the enhanced Adonis, in the words of the Chief Executive Officer, "tells it like it is."

Angelica and Bobo competed with each other with childish gluttony, to see who could eat more jelly donuts and drink more Coke. As the bubbles fizzed, there were excited burps, hiccups and snorts of laughter. Then Angelica suddenly realized she was almost exceeding her capacity.

She hurried over to the table where the two adults were sharing a pot of coffee and shop talk.

"Ms Schick," Angelica blurted out, "I need to go to the bathroom."

Ms Pinkney recognized the pretty little girl's frown of anguish as an urgent plea for help, smiled indulgently and promptly guided her to the nearest Comfort Station, one whose door was inscribed STAFF—LADIES.

Once Angelica had relieved her body, she enjoyed looking around, appreciating the suite's sumptuousness. Opposite the cubicles, there was a row of marble wash-basins with brightly lighted make-up mirrors, and open shelves of all sorts of cosmetics and *eaux de toilette*; and next to that stood a large, chrome-plated dispenser of condoms. Because it was there for the convenience of the ladies of the staff, the prophylactics were accessible without coins.

Nibbling her lower lip in concentration beyond childishness, Angelica considered the condoms on offer. There were colorless ones and others of different pastel colors, with the names of various fruits.

She chose Strawberry, and pressed the appropriate button.

7

While Cynthia was upstairs in her dressing room, titivating herself for dinner with the Ersdales, Arnold and Angelica were waiting in the living room, doing their best to enjoy a Happy Hour of unpredictable duration.

On special occasions, Cynthia was inclined to take her time deciding what to wear, and then deciding to wear something else. Dinner with Elwood and Jeanette was only a Grade B special occasion, but Cynthia was always determined to look Grade A, so that people like the Ersdales would feel Grade C. They were not Old Annapolitans and their money was not Old Money, but they had an awful lot of New Money. Their house was beyond heritage antiquity, on the fringe of the city, but it was twice as big as the Bosworths' place, and there was a heated pool. There was no Ersdale summer house in Martha's Vineyard, but they had a guarded condominium for winter vacations in Palm Beach. Cynthia could not help feeling somewhat challenged.

Arnold, at Cynthia's request, was already attired in the guise of Successful Author, in a Donegal tweed jacket with unnecessary extra pocket flaps to show it was custom-made, cavalry twill trousers and dark-brown suede loafers, without tassels. He looked quite authentic, but how she wished she could persuade him to smoke a pipe, or at least carry one. Early in their marriage, she had requested a beard—nothing excessive, little more than designer stubble. He had surprised and irritated her by resisting the suggestion. There were still details she wished to improve.

Arnold was leaning back in a deep armchair beside the fieldstone fireplace. No logs burned, but it was brightened by a vase of spring flowers. Angelica, still in her school T-shirt and jeans, was behind the bamboo bar, concocting their drinks. He smiled with fond indulgence at her expression of dedication. Her drink was her usual 7-Up plus a spoonful of vanilla icecream, but his required special care.

"Easy on the vermouth," he reminded her.

"Oh, Daddy, I know. Don't spoil it." By "it," she meant her belief in his confidence that she had learnt how to make a proper vodka martini.

"Sorry," he said. It wasn't easy to realize how quickly she was growing up.

She stirred the ice in the shaker's base until it misted with cold, and did not let any ice slip into his Steuben cocktail glass. For a moment they were silent, as she began slicing peel from a lemon. The oil of the zest was an important ingredient. He could not refrain from uttering another warning.

"Please, Angel, do be careful. I've sharpened that knife and—"

"'—it's as sharp as a razor.'"

"Well, yes. It is. If it slipped, you could give yourself a very nasty cut."

"OK, I was careful. Look."

She placed the small, glittering steel knife down on the bar and held up the short strip of lemon peel for his approval, before twisting it between forefingers and thumbs and dropping it delicately into his martini.

"I know I sometimes fuss," he apologized.

"Only because you love me?"

He grinned and nodded.

"Because I love you."

"All right then."

Angelica might well have been able to squeeze out a few more drops of affection, like fragrance from the lemon, but the conversation was halted by the dramatic entrance of Cynthia in her role of diva. She was elegant in black silk, emeralds and a cloud of sweet muskiness; and, of course, her brow was corrugated with impatience. She wanted to be a bit late; however, she did not want to be too late. She already had her sable draped over one arm.

"Come on,' she said. "Let's go."

"Ready in a minute," he assured her. "Angie has just made me a drink."

"What are you doing—training her to be a bartender?"

"Angie would be an excellent bartender. She has a way with a martini."

"Very funny," Cynthia said, in a very unamused manner. "Angelica is nine years old. Anyway, it's getting late. Leave the drink. There'll be enough where we're going. Possibly mixed even better than hers."

Detecting the probability of an unpleasant conflict, Arnold turned to Angelica with an apologetic shrug.

"Too bad, poppet. I wouldn't want to upset the Ersdales. I'll have to take a rain check."

Angelica didn't say a word. She only glared at her stepmother's back, as she flounced from the room.

Arnold was slowly following when he felt a tug at his sleeve.

"I have a present for you," Angelica said, handing him the small envelope from Adonis.

Recognizing what it was, he hurriedly thrust it into a pocket.

"Strawberry ones," she told him. "Why do they name those things after different fruits?"

8

Even on early acquaintance, Elwood ("Woody") Ersdale made a macho ceremony of greeting. He did the double-handed handshake and the embrace and back-patting that had come with the olive oil and omerta from Palermo to New York, Hollywood and Las Vegas—eventually to every place where the movers and shakers did business and socialized, especially in the Nation's capital, in the White House. The ostensibly warm intimacy of the gangsters' gestures was admired and emulated by all those who learned decorum from television.

When Arnold disengaged his right hand from the two strong hands that shook it, he knew that his failure to offer a responsive squeeze was something of a gaffe, and he knew that his passiveness in Elwood's friendly bear hug might have hurt, perhaps offended, a less confident host. Elwood's confidence was proclaimed by a moss-green velvet smoking jacket with black silk lapels. The smooth, firm, ruddy, massaged meatiness of his face seemed to exude an aroma of wellbeing. He had a thick, brutal nose; dark-yellow hair that curled abundantly over the ears and on the nape of the neck, and watery grey eyes that bulged as if he were continuously, agreeably astonished to find that he was rich in a rich country, where a dollar was still worth almost a dollar. He was not about to shrink from one of Jeanette's new coterie of so-called intellectuals, least of all a man in tweed who wrote stories about a squirrel.

The moment passed without cooling the welcome. After all, friendliness was Elwood's stock in trade—Woody's stock in trade. He was the president of his own small, elite advertising consultancy and a registered Washington lobbyist. A Californian corporation at the heart of the military-industrial complex was his only client. One was quite enough, for its annual budget in contribution to "national defense" (the best defense is attack) was measured in billions. A small fraction of that amount was sufficient to make Elwood a wealthy man, with ample funds left over for bending legislators to his client's purposes.

Elwood always gave good value. One of his most useful, tame Senators, Charlie Brocklehurst, whose wife and he appreciated the finer things in life, such as vacations in five-star tropical resorts, was able to provide constructive guidance to committees dealing with justice and the ways and means of the aerospace program. He also had easy, informal access to the Vice-President, which meant a lot to Jeanette. The relationship encouraged her to hope, not altogether unreasonably, that she might get close one day to the President and his First Lady. Elwood's lobbying for armed confrontation with foreign terrorists could bring about some nice domestic spin-offs.

Jeanette, Cynthia couldn't help noticing, was looking slightly terrific, wearing her glossy brunette hair up, augmented by a cunningly integrated hairpiece; a long, white gown of exquisite simplicity, except for silver filigree embroidery at the neck, the ends of the sleeves and the hem; a ring bearing a solitaire the size of a sugar lump; and a brilliant hostess smile. The whiteness of the whites of her eyes, the white of her teeth and the white of her gown did much to emphasize her café-au-lait tan.

"What stunning shoes!" Cynthia exclaimed. She and Jeanette had been friends for several weeks, since they had met at one of Jeanette's soirées for writers and artists, and they were already experts at bringing each other down with the smallest of compliments.

Jeanette glanced down at her shoes as if she had never considered them seriously before.

"Oh, thank you, darling. Do you like them?"

Jeanette placed her right cheek close to Cynthia's in the customary non-kiss kiss. The rituals in the entrance hall having been completed, the two couples were able to move farther inside, to get at the Dom Perignon, the champagne of choice of the stars of the novels of Harold Robbins and Jackie Collins. Their blockbusters are full of glitterati giving good head and good champagne.

"Arnold," Jeanette said with a smile of unembarrassment, "I have a confession to make. There isn't another guest, that special fan." She paused and searched his face for a reaction, but there didn't seem to be one. "That special fan's me."

"That's very flattering," Cynthia was quick to comment. "Isn't that flattering, Arnold?"

"Very."

"I've read all the Squidgy books," Jeanette vouchsafed.

"I tried to get one on Talking Books," Elwood said, "to listen to in the car, to find out what she was going on about, but Amazon didn't have any."

"There aren't any yet," Arnold admitted.

"That figures then. Now, who's for some Dom Perignon?"

As usual when the Ersdales had guests, even on the smallest scale, the caterer had arranged dinner. There was nothing daringly experimental about the menu, just Beluga caviar, terrapin bouillon, lobster Newburg and salad, crêpes Suzette and cheese.

"I thought it would be OK to have champagne all the way through," Elwood said, "but if you'd prefer something else just say the word."

Everything was of an excellence worthy of D.C.'s top-of-the-range expense-account restaurants.

"I know how people feel about smoking these days," he said near the end of the meal, "so, if you gals will excuse us, Arnold and me'll tip-toe over to my den for coffee and cigars and et cetera, and you can have your coffee and a chat in the lounge."

In a cosy room panelled in dark walnut, with a bar and an outsize screen suitable for major sports events, Elwood proffered Armagnac or a single-malt Scotch and a box of indecently long Upmann cigars, whose bands were personalized with the Ersdale monogram.

"There was a time when it wasn't easy to get Havana cigars," he said. "But even right after the Bay of Pigs and the Missile Crisis—long before our time—J.F.K, had to have his Havana cigars." Elwood wickedly tapped a conspiratorial forefinger against the side of his nose. "In Washington, like the committee says, there's always ways and means."

9

"Rhinoplasty, implants, liposuction, nip and tuck," Jeanette intoned, as though summarizing her whole adult career. "Refinement, plumping up, slimming down. That's all very well."

While Elwood, without having to think too hard, was holding forth on foreign affairs, potential trouble spots and the cost of pre-emption versus the long-term escalating cost of doing nothing, and Arnold was muzzily admiring the ash on his cigar and hardly thinking at all, their wives, who had drunk not much champagne, were now sipping coffee and digestifs of cranberry juice from miniature chalices of pale-blue Venetian glass and contemplating matters of more immediate personal relevance.

"I'm not knocking the cosmetic surgeons," Jeanette said, "or the dermatologists. D'you know, there was a time when I had *freckles*!"

"They've done a great job," Cynthia politely observed.

"Thanks. Sure, I owe them. They helped me along the way. I have a cuter nose, rounder tits, leaner thighs and a firmer ass than I had when I was starting out. If I didn't have, I doubt Woody would've looked twice. He says I present an iconic image. He can take me anywhere. All right, but isn't there more to life? My shrink says to really be content within myself I should make sure I don't neglect my inner child. Everyone has an inner child, he says, which most of them often don't ever think about."

"So what's one supposed to do exactly?"

"One of the troubles with the present contemporary Zeitgeist is people are always trying to come on as wise guys. You know? Quoting cartoons out of *The New Yorker* and what Jay Leno said in his monologue last night and all that, instead of looking at the world with their own eyes. My shrink says you have to peel away the outer layers of the onion."

"Hmm."

Jeanette moved her chair a little closer to Cynthia's and assumed an expression that was meant to be bright, cheerful and absolutely candid.

"I asked you two here this evening for a special reason," she said.

"Yes?"

"In addition to our friendship, of course. I have a great idea for a children's book. It's about a girl who goes to a magic school for wizards. It'll be a great story and a great motion picture. I'm willing to let Arnold in on it."

"How do you mean?"

"A collaboration. I'll provide the idea and Arnold can put it into words, the way he's good at. And here's the thing: I've already talked Woody into the deal. He'll put up some real money. Whatever Arnold's publisher gives him for a book, Woody'll pay double, so Arnold and me will be able to split it down the middle, fifty-fifty. How does that grab you?"

In the den, conversation had tightened from the international and the national to the personal and particular.

"I'd like your opinion," Elwood said. "Frankly, between us,

what do you think of the latest surgery on Jeanette's figure? The new implants."

Arnold shifted uneasily from buttock to buttock and looked up at the chandelier.

"She's very attractive," he muttered, smiling to confirm his sincerity.

"Don't bullshit me. Give it to me straight. You don't think she's had her specialist overdo the embonpoint?"

Arnold contrived a look of blank non-commitment, hoping for guidance.

"I like tits as much as the next man," Elwood declared with locker-room heartiness. But then he winced as if he had bitten into a wedge of lemon. "Most of us like big, I admit, but there's a limit. Jeanette is on the verge of hillbilly size. I'm looking for Senator Brocklehurst to fix me up with a Freedom Medal—that's the best a civilian can get—and I'm afraid there's a danger if Jeanette begins to look like a Country and Western chanteuse some of the neo-conservatives might.... What I'm saying is, any accusation of vulgarity could screw up my chances."

Elwood laid a hairy paw on Arnold's knee in a perfectly normal man-to-man signal of confidentiality. "Really, Arnold, I'm in the market for a high-profile charitable cause that would raise my dignity quotient. I was considering going the UNICEF route. You know about kids. What do you think?"

In the lounge, Cynthia did her best to encourage Jeanette without actually making any promises.

"I know Arnold is always on the look-out for ideas. The best plan is for you to talk with him yourself, in person. I could set up a meeting for the two of you. You could come over for eleven o'clock morning coffee. He's going to New York tomorrow. How about Thursday?"

"Oh, Cynthia, you're very dear. Would You do that? I'd appreciate it. I want Elwood to see I have a serious side." Jeanette frowned. "You don't think my breasts are too big now, do you?"

"Not at all," Cynthia kindly assured her. "Men are said to want them like that."

"Woody and me always call them tits," Jeanette said with a tinkling laugh. "He confesses he's a tit man. But the other evening, after a few aperitifs, he said that these aren't the tits he married. He admires their shape, and he approves of me being attractive to other men, up to a point. But he complains I'm beginning to feel unreal."

In the car on the way home, Cynthia outlined Jeanette's literary proposal.

"Of course, she's a moron," Cynthia said "but there's huge financial potential. You could name your price. She wants people to think she's into culture. Jeanette a writer! Elwood'd like the sound of that on Capitol Hill. For a wife with a classy reputation, the sky's the limit. You could give her top billing. Better still, you could have the book published under her name alone."

"Yes," Arnold said with an ominous chuckle. "Quite a concept. A girl goes to a magic school for wizards. Jeanette could call her Harriet Potter, and could get all the credit. I myself would want no part of it."

"You and your goddamn squirrel," Cynthia said, bringing dialogue temporarily to a close.

When they got home, Arnold went up to Angelica's bedroom. She was asleep. He stood by the head of her bed, adoring her golden hair, long eyelashes, peachy cheeks, Cupid's-bow upper lip and the curled fingers of one hand at the silken hem of her pink blanket. Though her eyes were shut, she somehow felt his gaze, and awoke.

"Daddy!" she delightedly exclaimed.

"Sorry I disturbed you," he said, smoothing her hair back with a gentle caress. "I only wanted to give you a goodnight kiss."

She held out her arms, and he kissed her forehead.

"Daddy," she said.

"Yes, pumpkin?"

"Does Cynthia want to have a baby?"

"Really, Angie! What a question! The answer is I don't know."

"If you don't want a baby, those things I gave you can make sure she doesn't have one or give you a horrible disease."

He marvelled at her innocence, her directness.

10

Naomi Swartkop, the Editorial Director and Vice-President of Varoom!, the Children's Fiction Division of Croesus Communications, the world's fastest developing multimedia conglomerate, activated her electronic desk diary and an elocutionized contralto reminded her she had Arnold Bosworth for lunch at twelve o'clock.

"Makes me sound like a cannibal," Ms Swartkop said drily to her Personal Assistant, a young man in attendance at a conveniently close desk almost half the size of hers. He chuckled appreciatively, because chuckling appreciatively was a crucial function of his job.

"Better than if he had you for lunch, Ms S," he said, gratuitously laboring the jest.

"Get me a table for two at The Lucullan," she commanded, unsmiling. She did the one-liners; there was no call for repartee.

He was savvy enough to seem chastened.

"Yes, Ms Swartkop."

He made up for the inferiority of his position by speaking arrogantly on the telephone to the restaurant's maître d'.

Thirty-eight floors below in the Croesus Building, Arnold was in the white-marble lobby, twenty minutes early, going through the procedure of security clearance, which, he always thought, must be like preparing for jail. As instructed, though he did not need to be told what to do, he looked straight into the lens of the automatic camera, and submitted a docile hand to the black-uniformed guard at the reception desk for finger-printing. The guard gave Arnold a laminated card to pin to a lapel of his chalk-striped navy blue suit. However, after the guard spoke briefly on his phone, it became apparent that the clearance and the card were unnecessary.

"You don't have to go up," he said. "Ms Swartkop will come down at twelve. You can take a seat." He indicated a row of chairs alongside the wall opposite the elevators. "There's reading material on the table," he added kindly.

Arnold had been an established Varoom! author since the time, until recently, when the imprint had been less dramatically called Croesus Children's Books. But Naomi was up there, and he was down here. He was not allowed to forget who had the power and who was at its disposal.

The Varoom! catalogue for Summer and Fall was as splendid as ever, but to Arnold it was a disappointment. In past seasons, he had been accustomed to having a whole page of his own, with an illustration in color from the latest Squidgy title and a photograph of himself, with chin cupped in hand as though deep in thought, at a desk with a background of books. He was searching with shrinking hope for Bosworth, Arnold, and Squidgy in the backlist, when he heard the rapid click-click of high heels on marble and his editor's voice.

"Hi!" Naomi said. He stood up and she shook his hand. "Trust you haven't been waiting long." Arnold knew she knew how long.

"I was a bit ahead of time," he admitted. "The cab driver was

Iranian, but he was able to find the way from Penn Station."

"All of fourteen blocks."

"The new drivers aren't all ignorant. This one spoke fluent American. He said he was an orthopaedist before he came over."

"So you were lucky, even if he isn't."

The ice having been broken, she led him from the building.

"See if you can get lucky again," she suggested. He started waving at yellow taxis and soon stopped one.

"We're going to The Lucullan," she said, "if that's all right." The Lucullan, of course. Where else? He had read that The Lucullan was currently the most expensive, most-difficult-to-get-a-table-at restaurant in Manhattan.

She gave the Nigerian driver the name of the restaurant, the street address and the name of the closest avenue, and he took off with a furious squeal of tires.

"Sometimes if you tell them everything and they already know it they get mad," she said with a calm smile, amused by primitive psychology.

"You can't win," Arnold said, and the cliché caused her to give him a sharp look. She devoted herself to the conviction that she could win, always. He made no further attempt at conversation for the rest of the short journey. She was already making him nervous. Even during his heyday, Naomi's nicely poised androgyny, simultaneously attractive and deterrent to men and women alike, her cropped brown hair, her handsomely wide-set brown eyes, her Katharine Hepburn facial bone structure and the chic mannishness of her suits charmed him yet made him feel uncomfortable, as a snake is said to charm a rabbit before paralyzing it with fear.

Because Naomi lunched there several times a week and her tips were lavish enough to be considered bribes, the maître d' put on his most oleaginous French accent and personally guided them to her usual table. As he smoothly inserted a chair beneath her person, he paid tribute to the fine Spring weather, as if paying her a compliment.

"Thank you, Antoine," she said with a regal nod, though his name at home in Hackensack was Kevin.

Arnold accepted the Menu du Jour, a calligraphic work of art in sepia ink on parchment. He was about to study it, when Naomi announced their agenda.

"This is going to be a cutting-edge power lunch for blue-sky brainstorming your next era of creativity," she said with a straight face. "Big time." Then she gave him her special smile, the open one with lots of teeth. "Don't be alarmed—only kidding. This restaurant is no think tank."

As he had read Freud's treatise on *The Joke and Its Relation to the Unconscious*, he knew that every mirth-provoking gambit, from the clown's thwack with a slapstick to the wisenheimer's verbal banana skin, requires a victim, who may or may not join in the ensuing hilarity. She endeavored to put his mind at rest. "I don't really talk like that, Arnold. All I mean is I want to toss around some ideas about what we at Varoom! feel you should direct your talent to next."

"That would be very—" he began. She flashed an interjectory smile and continued.

"But first and foremost," she assured him, "Lunch is lunch. Chef Raymond is from Lyons, France. He has won every award there is over there. His pheasant pâté's to die for. I wish I weren't so strict with myself: I'm watching my intake. But don't let me hold you back. What'll you have to drink?"

"What are you drinking?" he asked cautiously.

"Me, I'm going for the papaya juice. But they make a delicious papaya daiquiri, I've been told—good for a sunny day like today."

Arnold decided he must assert himself by resisting the recommendation.

"What I'd really like," he said, "is a Jack Daniels on the rocks." Her flinch was imperceptible, but her smile was noticeably less brilliant than before.

"A he-man's choice!" she said. In fencing terms, her comment was a riposte. There was no getting around the fact, Arnold warned himself: she was a bitch.

11

He was feeling better about her and himself by the time she was engaged in dissecting a grilled sole and he was vigorously sawing into the pink interiors of two thick lamb chops. For twenty minutes or so she had not uttered a single snide remark, even about the people at other tables. Enabling him to relax, she enabled him to admire the silken gloss of her short brown hair, the uprightness of her posture in her purple silk suit, the flawless pallor of her complexion, the surgical precision with which she was gradually disclosing the fish's skeleton. While she took sips of chilled water imported from a Swiss mountain spring, he was fortified by swallows of red Burgundy. He felt that parity had been achieved, as though they were a man and woman simply enjoying lunch together. The illusion was short-lasting.

"Is the Beaune OK?" she inquired.

"Yes. Excellent."

"The Lucullan is said to have established one of the best cellars in New York." When she had invited him to choose his wine, the leather-bound list had impressed him with the enormity of the prices. In this way, she reminded him that she was the benefactor, he the beneficiary.

"Have you ever wondered about my name?" she asked. The

abrupt change of subject and the unexpectedness of the question were unsettling. What was she getting at? She was always getting at something subtler than the meringue and mocha icecream on his dessert plate.

"It's an unusual name," he ventured.

"Only in its Americanized form. Maybe Swartkop was the way it was written down by some immigration officer on Ellis Island. Those guys sometimes had difficulties spelling foreign names, and my great-grandfather probably had to take what was given. But there've been plenty of families who were able to keep their names unchanged. The Schwarzkopf I specially admired was 'Stormin' Norman'. Remember him?"

Arnold confessed that he didn't.

"General Schwarzkopf was the commander of Operation Desert Storm, in the First Gulf War. I was a sophomore at Barnard then, majoring in English and American literature. A lot of us got a big kick out of his daily media briefings on CNN. I liked to believe there was a genetic connection."

Arnold nodded, waiting for more.

"You must have been at school around that time," she said.

"Yes. I was at Hopkins. Political science, before I switched. Not much help when I—"

"I was proud to have virtually the same name," Naomi went on. "The general had great presence. He was a big man, wearing immaculate combat fatigues in desert colors. He had all the facts and figures at his fingertips. And he had charm and the humor of the sharpest stand-up. He *humanized* the smart bomb. His comments on the air-to-ground film footage were out of this world. You had to laugh when he showed an Iraqi truck-driver being blown up on a bridge."

Arnold knew she would soon get to the point.

"People of all ages are entertained by shocks like that," she said. "It would be hypocritical to pretend they aren't. I learned a valuable lesson from the good general, and it has been confirmed and re-enforced by my analysis of the game machines in the amusement arcades. The games that children really go for are the ones with the highest speeds, the loudest explosions, the most violent fights. Kids don't want old custard-pie-in-the-face comedy. They certainly don't want cute. What makes them scream with laughter is the sight of a game in which men like gorillas are beaten to a pulp. Which brings us to the purpose of this meeting. Let us consider the decline and fall of your Squidgy the Squirrel."

Arnold felt a sudden stabbing pain of acid indigestion.

"'Decline and fall'?" he repeated. "I still get fan mail from children saying how much they love Squidgy."

"Don't tell me you think those letters are genuine," Naomi said with a snort of incredulity. "Teachers—especially the dogmatic spinsters who used to be in charge of educational policy on the primary level—have always dictated children's opinions and most of the letters too. Until not very long ago, the moral and literary standards of children's books, with not many exceptions, have been conservative. But haven't you heard? Queen Victoria is dead. We don't need any more anthropomorphic tales about our lovable little furry friends. Kids prefer the don't-give-a-damn grasshopper to the industrious ant. They would rather be the flashy hare than the plodding tortoise. Give us a break, Arnold—it's time for Squidgy's funeral."

Arnold felt a spurt of indignation. Naomi was so wrong, so unfair! Croesus had made millions out of his Squidgy books. It was true that sales were not what they used to be, but still.... He put down his spoon and fork with a clatter.

"Do you mean you got me up to New York only to say Varoom!

and I are through? What about my present contract?"

"There, there, Arnold." She patted the back of his hand, as if pacifying a fretful child. "You should read the small print. But there'll be a generous ex gratia compensation. Don't have a tantrum. This isn't the end of our beautiful relationship. However, it is definitely time to move forward. We recognize that children are determined to get the entertainment they really want. That's what the internet is for."

12

"How are they supposed to select stories of quality without guidance?"

"Come off it, Arnold. We're not crusaders for art. Publishing is a commercial enterprise. We're in the business of turning over product in meganumbers. We're in trade to make money—money for our shareholders, money for you and me. Do you think those royalty checks we've been sending you every six months have been in recognition of your artistic sensibility?"

"There was a time when publishers cared about books."

"We still do, particularly when the people out there in California care as well."

Arnold picked up his fork and cracked his meringue into smaller and smaller fragments.

"We at Varoom! admire you as a craftsman, Arnold. We like the way we don't have to fix your grammar and syntax. In the children's new world of sex and violence, there's a place for you, and we are proposing to enable you to find it."

She ordered two coffees.

"There's one innovative line of development you probably don't want to become involved in. I know the way you feel about originality, but there's going to be very nice money in it. We're going to vamp up a few well-known children's classics that are now in the public domain, give them contemporary oomph. Imagine the potential of *The Wind in The Willows*, *Treasure Island*, the Alice books. Think how we can bring them to life!"

"*The Wind in The Willows* already ends with violence," Arnold pointed out. "The liberation of Toad Hall from the stoats and weasels. And there's enough violence in *Treasure Island*. I assume it's sex you're planning to add. I've always thought those River Bankers ought to come out of the closet, and Long John Silver obviously was a pedophile. Then—"

"There'd be nothing wrong if Mole and Ratty turned out to be gay or at least an irritable, frustrated Odd Couple," Naomi reasoned. "Anyway, I suspected you might be too frivolous for the project, and now I'm sure I was right. Too bad, because you have the technical ability for the job."

"Do you think Toad got a thrill out of dressing up in the washerwoman's clothes to escape from prison? There's a broad hint of transvestism there."

"All right, Arnold. Drop it. We have already commissioned a wonderful, sincere Sarah Lawrence grad student to take on *Alice in Wonderland*. She's very enthused about the possibilities of making some valid statements. You have a daughter, don't you, Arnold?"

"Angelica's nine years old."

"I bet she already thinks Lewis Carroll's a drag, in the old-fashioned state of his works."

"He isn't one of her favorite authors," Arnold had to concede.

"He could be when Alice makes fun comments on some relevant topics of today. But there you go, frowning again."

He was thinking of condoms.

"Cheer up! We have a completely fresh idea for you," Naomi promised. "Have a liqueur with your coffee."

13

"You said you'd be beat by the time you got home," Cynthia said, her nose creased as though by an unpleasant odor. "I didn't expect you to look this beat. Did you two indulge in a bit of *cinq-à-sept*?"

"A bit of what?"

"Oh, I forgot you've never been to Paris. It's what the French call their traditional hours of adultery. Five to seven is such a romantic time of the evening, isn't it? What I mean is, did you have to screw your Mrs Scharwzkopf?"

"Her name is Swartkop," Arnold said. "And don't be ridiculous. It was a very serious conference."

"What's publishing's equivalent of the casting couch? Does she keep a suite at The Regency? The Algonquin isn't what it was."

"Don't be ridiculous, Cynthia. It's been a rough day. I'm not in the mood for your—"

"Right. Let's be very serious. How many drinks did you have in the train?"

Arnold looked up at the ceiling, appealing for help to preserve his patience, but no help was forthcoming.

"Listen," he said. "I'm tired. If you don't feel ready to hear what today was about, I'll try to get through to you tomorrow. As a matter of fact, Cynthia, you look rather tired yourself. Beautiful, of course. Elegant—new dress? But tired. And somewhat peeved. So shall we go to bed? If you wish, I can sleep in the guest room."

"You listen, buster," she replied. "This was Belle' s half-day off. While you were gallivanting about in Manhattan, I was stuck here in Annapolis. I had to feed the brat. And I get tired wondering how you intend to get hold of all the money we need."

"Don't talk like that about Angelica."

"I had to give the little angel her supper. She may have a terrific

IQ but she still doesn't know how—or chooses to pretend not to know—how to operate the microwave."

Belle, their live-out housekeeper and maid of all work, was a good cook who cooked real food. Cynthia refused to make any culinary effort beyond defrosting, thawing and heating meals that were prefabricated, and even those simple, mechanical operations provoked in her a resentment that permeated the whole house with negative vibrations.

"As I'm sure you must care," she said, "I had a Caesar's salad and an iced tea with Jeanette at The Poop Deck. She's moving closer every day. At least I got out of the goddamn house for a couple of hours. Or should I say goshdarned? But let's not talk about me. How was your lunch? Where was it? What did you have? What was your hostess wearing? Do you mind letting me know what the fuck the meeting produced and what's in it for me? I'm all ears. Why wait till tomorrow?"

"If you'd let me get a few words in edgewise," Arnold said. "We had lunch at The Lucullan—yes, of course, The Lucullan; the check must have been huge. No I don't know exactly how huge. We'll skip the menu. Naomi was dressed in some kind of purple suit; I didn't read the label. What the fuck the fucking meeting produced was the death of Squidgy."

At last Cynthia was earnestly attentive, but managed to withhold tears.

"So you're out?"

"No, I'm not out. Squidgy is. Naomi says Varoom! will give me an even bigger and better contract."

Cynthia immediately appeared to be about ten years younger. Arnold gave her a weary smile.

"All I have to do is tour the country for a while to understand the contemporary child's psyche. Then I have to produce a book that Naomi and her henchpersons approve of, the first book in an endless series enlivened by plenty of childish sex and violence. I'll be leaving on this tour as soon as a few arrangements have been made. It won't be a long tour. It'll be extensive but not long in duration. I'll be making quick visits to a variety of venues from sea to shining sea, investigating all aspects of the culture of the modern American child. Total immersion, total concentration will be required."

"My, how clever of you, darling," Cynthia said in her nastiest sweet manner. "But if you think I'm coming along to hold your hand you're out of your mind."

Arnold attempted to look downcast, but he was glad he did not have to tell her that Naomi had insisted he undertake the expedition alone.

"That's our hope for the future," he said. "Right now, it's time for our nightcaps. If you'd like to go ahead upstairs, I'll bring you your hot chocolate in a few minutes."

After she had swallowed her "Barbie doll" capsules, he went down to his so-called library to take his, in the usual generous snifter of brandy.

Eventually, yawning and scratching his scalp, he opened Angie's door for a goodnight glimpse. Once again, his fond gaze somehow caused her to open her eyes, and kisses were exchanged.

"Daddy," she murmured in a sleepy voice, "what did Cynthia mean when she asked did you screw Naomi Swartkop? Does screw mean the same as that other word? You didn't, did you?"

Angelica was an expert eavesdropper.

14

Under the shower a few mornings later, Arnold massaged himself with an abundant lather and rejoiced in the prospect of leaving his wife, if only for a couple of weeks. In his enthusiastic bathroom baritone, occasionally soaring into the tenor range, he sang of the Owl and the Pussy Cat. As Edward Lear noted in his lyrical poem about them, they were well provided for when they embarked in their beautiful pea-green boat. Arnold did justice to the imperishable words: "They took some honey/ And plenty of money/ Wrapped up in a five-pound note." Naomi had guaranteed the full support of Varoom!'s vast resources. With her say-so, the accountants were bound to concede that the stratosphere was the limit.

Some of the best writers for children, Arnold happily reflected, were crazy, more or less, now and then. Edward Lear, in the most beguiling fashion, was certifiably gaga. Spike Milligan, vertiginously manic, then abysmally depressed, periodically had to withdraw from the mediocrity of convention for psychiatric therapy. Maurice Sendak was most delightful when inspired by surrealist delusions, *Where The Wild Things Are* and *In The Night Kitchen*. Alcohol sometimes over-excited James Thurber. *New Yorker* editors and his own blindness irritated him. He was relieved by empathy with children. He recognized that in every child there is a lot of Walter Mitty yearning for glamorous heroics.

There are characters in the dream-worlds of children' s fiction who achieve reasonableness. Beatrix Potter reported that Peter Rabbit's mother sensibly advised her son to stay clear of Mr McGregor's garden. "Your father had an accident there," she said. "He was put in a pie by Mrs McGregor." Tomi Ungerer's dear little Zeralda, in *Zeralda's Ogre*, was a practical pragmatist who perceived that the way to an ogre's heart was through his belly. She cooked him such elaborate, delicious banquets that he gave up his antisocial habit of devouring children. It was not her fault that when they got married their son inherited a desire for cannibalism.

Drying himself with gymnastic vigor, Arnold felt so pleased

by the way things were shaping up that he was unable to refrain from shouting "Hallelujah!" He should not have been surprised, on returning to their bedroom, when Cynthia said she wanted to know what took him so long and how come he had flipped. His explanation for shouting was evasive.

"I had a great shower" was all he would say.

15

There was an interval between the rains of April, and the sunshine was warm, but not too warm, so Arnold walked Angelica to school. She was in a talkative mood, as though this might be a farewell conversation. He was already packed to go that evening.

"On this trip," she said, "you'll probably meet lots of ladies, won't you?"

"I suppose I will. Many of the teachers in the schools I'm planning to visit will be women. I'll talk with some women librarians. I want to meet parents, and half of them are mothers. You don't mind my meeting women, do you?"

Angie ignored the question. After a thoughtful pause, she said:

"If Cynthia left you—"

"What makes you say that?"

"I hear you fighting."

"We don't fight. In every marriage, there are sometimes disagreements. We talk our way through them. That's not fighting."

"Well, I'm just saying *if.* Would you get married again?"

"That is what is known as a hypothetical question, honeybun. It's a very big *if.* I don't think she would want to leave us. She likes being where she is."

"She likes buying things with your money. She's always on about things she wants you to get for her."

Arnold did his best to laugh.

"Everyone wants things, Angie. You do too, I know."

"Bobo and me—Bobo and I—have long talks."

"You're very close, aren't you? That's nice."

"Bobo says since the divorce her mother has joined the Annapolis Chapter of Divorcées Anonymous. They have buffet suppers with lectures and discussions."

"Lively ones, I bet."

"Bobo's mother got to keep Bobo and she's told her a lot about marriage. For instance, Bobo's mother says men stink."

"Rather prejudiced."

"Bobo's mother has girl friends now. That's what she calls them. They're not really girls as such."

"As such" and "per se" were two of Bobo's latest expressions, so, of course, they were Angelica's as well. "They're ladies her own age or even older. Bobo's mother says she and her girl friends see eye to eye the way a lady and a man can't see. She and her girl friends have a lot in common. She gets together with one of them almost every day. They go shopping and have meals together and everything. They go on vacation trips. Bobo says they never fight at all."

"Good for them" was Arnold's only comment, heavy with irony.

"Bobo says when we grow up she and I ought to live together. She's going to be a lawyer and make plenty of money. She says she's going to specialize in big-deal divorces and take all those pigs to the cleaners. She says we could afford for me to be creative. I could be some kind of designer. What do you think?"

"I'm sure you'll be very good at whatever you decide to do. Anyway, you have plenty of time to consider all your options."

"I'll be ten in four months."

"That's not very old."

"Then, before I know it, I'll be a teenager."

"True."

"I want to be a writer like you. It would be wonderful to write children's books. The only trouble is you've already had all the best ideas anyone could possibly have."

"Don't worry about that," he said, patting her shoulder and giving it an encouraging little squeeze. "There are countless better ideas floating about out there."

"When we grow up," Angie said, reverting to long-term ambitions and anxieties, "Bobo says she's not going to let any men 'do it' to her. She calls it 'doing it.'"

"Perhaps she'll feel quite different when the time comes."

"You mean when the hormones kick in?"

Once again, she shook him.

"Ms Schick hasn't yet done hormones in Sex," Angie said, "but I know what they are. Bobo and I have done some outside reading. She says some of it's enough to make you throw up, but I don't mind it. Bobo says as soon as she leaves home for good the first thing she's going to do is have a hysterectomy. That's when they take out your uterus and all that stuff, so you can't ever have your insides cluttered up with kids."

"What a terrible idea," Arnold said. "How sad. It's lucky your mother didn't do that. There'd be no Angie."

"Bobo says her mother sometimes gets very depressed. When she gets extra depressed she says she's going to take an overdose. But her doctor has given her some new pills that make her happy, so that's OK."

There was another brief silence, except for the sound of their footsteps, walking in time along the sidewalk. John Paul Jones Elementary was in sight.

"I feel sorry for Bobo not having you," Angie said, looking up at him so lovingly that he had to look straight ahead. Her devotion was unnervingly intense. He felt a moistening of his eyes. He swallowed. He said:

"You'll always be my daughter. I'll always be your father."

"Will you?" she demanded. "Promise? Whatever happens?"

"Whatever happens."

16

"Harlem first," Naomi Swartkop had suggested. Her suggestions were tantamount to commands. She issued them with ardor. Just mentioning the name of the place enabled her to believe in herself as a feel-good liberal. Demographics and other socio-economic indicators, she explained, convinced her that African-Americans should not be ignored.

"Our marketing people assure us that the ethnic neighborhoods are opening up in a big way," she assured Arnold. "Middle-class black is beautiful—a dynamic growth area of consumerism. African-Americans constitute approximately twelve per cent of the citizenry of these United States. That amounts to something like thirty million of them. Surveys reveal that most of their children are computer-literate by the age of five, and quite a few of them can read. Harlem is the capital of black America. Bill Clinton has his office on 125th Street, for heaven's sake. Toni Morrison, the first African-American Nobel laureate for literature, called Clinton 'the first black President this country ever had.' So let's go for black, Arnold—not exclusively, of course, but to a significant minor extent. The window is opening. I'm counting on you to push the envelope."

She was excited.

"Think of selling to domestic ethnics as a rehearsal for getting Varoom! into all of Asia. Looking at China and India et cetera, we're looking at billions of potential Varoom! readers. Billions,

Arnold! Publishing books for children has long ceased to be a genteel WASP hobby and the avocation of Jewish idealists. Beyond the Afros, the Hispanics and all the regular Americans here in our own backyard, we're going globally interracial. We're researching Muslims even, and not a day too soon—they're a population of huge human resources, world-wide. We have to put out books of universal appeal, not only for the nieces and nephews of maiden ladies in Boston. If the kids are downloading sex and violence, so be it; that's the area we should be at. Let's not admit lowest common denominator though; let us proclaim highest common factor, quality fiction that everybody wants, in easy-to-comprehend American English beyond social and national boundaries, books as tempting, assimilable and profit-generating as chicken nuggets.

"From where I sit," she went on, "it looks like every story should introduce one black in every eight characters—not only as a token walk-on but in a major secondary role, like an Oscar nominee for best supporting actor, with Terrence Howard's looks and Poitier's sincerity, if we want to penetrate the Harlem community and all the satellite communities that look to Harlem as a cultural paradigm.

"And remember, Arnold," she chided him, wagging an admonitory forefinger discomfortingly close to his face, "writing is not intellectual masturbation. It's an industry. It isn't your thoughts that count; it's the readers. We aren't publishing children's books to massage your ego. When I head for the Frankfurt Book Fair this fall, I have to be fully armed with innovative product, class scripts worthy of auction and promotion. Arnold, the fact is you have to get up off your ass."

She had gone on and on in this challenging vein. Her message was firmly imprinted in Arnold's awareness. In the days between the Lucullan conference and his departure from Annapolis, much to Cynthia's derisive contempt, he agitatedly riffled through many landmark works, such as Booker T. Washington's autobiography *Up From Slavery*, poems by Langston Hughes, Carl Van Vechten's novel *Nigger Heaven* (Arnold was astonished to see there was a time when a reputable publisher dared to print the N-word), Ralph Ellison's novel *Invisible Man* and James Baldwin's passionate polemic *The Fire Next Time*. There was no opportunity to read about Afrodite, the black goddess of love. For relief there were only the Uncle Remus tales. By the time Arnold was due to leave, he felt like Bre'er Rabbit about to encounter the Tar Baby of racism—the original one, not Toni Morrison's less playful adaptation.

As he waved goodbye and carried his suitcase out to the taxi, Cynthia sardonically smirked and Angelica wept hot tears. Each of them, in different ways, was about to prepare their fate.

17

Arnold decided to spend the first night of his research expedition in midtown Manhattan, to get himself together for a fresh, early start in Harlem.

He chose to stay at the St Regis, which, at 5th Avenue and 55th Street, is as midtown as you can get.

To begin with, he was feeling pleased with his organizational ability. Having checked in early in the evening, he went up to his room, had a leisurely bath, and dressed in the clothes he was to wear the following morning, a modest spring suit of light-grey tropical worsted, a pale-blue shirt and a burnt-sienna paisley tie. Rather subtle, that tie, he thought, congratulating himself at the mirror, as he adjusted the knot and the dimple below it. J. Alfred Prufrock couldn't have managed a knot any better. Arnold carefully disarranged a silk handkerchief of a different paisley pattern in his breast pocket, and combed his hair, and enjoyed a rare moment of confident self-esteem.

The euphoria did not last throughout a lonely dinner in the hotel restaurant. His twenty per cent tip was rewarded with thanks that seemed more formally subservient than friendly. He returned to his room.

The telephone at the other end was picked up after only three rings.

"Hello?" demanded Angelica.

"Hello, sweetie. It's me. That was quick."

"That's because I'm in the library—for the encyclopedia. We're doing the Civil War. The War between the States."

"Good girl. May I speak with your mother."

"She isn't my mother," she reminded him for about the thousandth time. "Cynthia's out. She's having dinner with her precious Ersdales. In Washington. They're talking about the adoption plan."

"The adoption plan?"

Angelica was dedicated to listening to other people's conversations, especially doing so at doors ajar and on telephone extensions, and she was good at remembering what she overheard.

"Jeanette says Mr Ersdale wants to adopt three five-year-old orphans, nice, quiet, obedient ones, cute ones, from underdeveloped countries in Africa and ... places like that—for one year. 'Kids of assorted colors' was what Jeanette told Cynthia."

Arnold did not pry into his daughter's sources of information. The range of her inside knowledge never ceased to surprise him, and he did not want to stem the flow.

"Did your—did Cynthia mention UNESCO?" he wondered.

"Yes. She and the Ersdales are crazy though, aren't they?"

"The United Nations are doing a great deal to help the Third World," he gently rebuked Angelica. "Adopting orphans is one way. All these wars leave millions of children without families and homes. I'm sure Mr Ersdale wants to do his best."

His best for Elwood Ersdale, Arnold thought. Adoption of orphans must be part of the public-relations campaign for the Freedom Medal.

"That's not all," Angelica said in the enthusiastic manner of a broadcaster exclusively reporting the latest bad news. "Jeanette is trying to persuade Cynthia to go along with the project. How would you like some orphans, Daddy? Black, brown and yellow."

Arnold imagined three strange five-year-olds running about in his desirable bijou residence, and how they would exacerbate relations, already fraught, between Cynthia and Angelica, not to mention his own self.

"So far," Angelica continued, "Cynthia says nothing doing. But you know she'd do anything to please the Ersdales, even though she hates children."

"As I've told you before, you just imagine she hates children," Arnold insisted. "But we can talk about the Ersdales' ideas when I come home."

"When's that going to be?"

"Quite soon. I'm only going to visit some schools to find out what children are thinking, the kind of books they would like and so on. At the moment, I called to ask Cynthia for some practical help. Nothing really very urgent. I can call back later."

"What is it you need, Daddy?"

"It was silly of me, but in my hurry I forgot to pack my sleeping capsules. I certainly don't want to spend half the nights awake. I have work to do. I want to be able to concentrate."

"The Barbies are on your desk, right by the phone." Evidently, Angelica picked up the bottle and read the label. "They're called *Oblivon*."

Angelica was very bright, Arnold realized, but she didn't understand absolutely everything about everything.

"I know what they're called," he said. "But what good will that do me? They're prescription drugs. I don't have my prescription with me."

"You can get one though, can't you? Isn't there a doctor where you're staying? Where *are* you staying?"

"I'm at the St Regis Hotel in New York, but only tonight, and I don't want to disturb a doctor this late. This isn't what anyone would call an emergency. Don't worry, honeybunch. I'll be OK."

"I know what you ought to do," Angelica said. For a 9-year-old girl, she could sound authoritatively maternal. "Do what you always do at home. Before bedtime, have a large glass of brandy. Have two. They'll put you to sleep."

"Angie, my pet," he said, smiling affectionately "I wonder where you got your IQ from. You're a genius."

"I got it from you."

"Very funny. Please tell Cynthia I called. Give her my love."

"If I remember," Angelica said, and hung up.

18

The King Cole Bar was quiet when Arnold got down there. The only merriment in the place was on the face of the merry old soul in the panoramic mural behind the bar. A few men were unmerrily drinking and there were many unoccupied seats. Arnold ordered a double Hine VSOP.

"An excellent choice, if I may say so, sir," said the bartender, who sounded English. Arnold tersely thanked him for the compliment without encouraging any further pleasantries. The bartender, well disciplined, move along the bar and devoted his attention to polishing an already well-polished glass.

The silence was total, except for the faint hum of something to do with refrigeration. Arnold regretted not having engaged the bartender in a conversation about the weather or the prospects for baseball or where one might expect the beginning of the Third World War. The opportunity had passed, but there would be another one if he decided to follow Angie's sensible advice about a second nightcap. The bartender set the fresh glass before Arnold with a deferential nod, and Arnold tried, without total success, to enliven his thanks with cordiality. The trouble was that he was anxious about the uncertainty of sleep, anxious about uncertainty of the future in general.

Again immersed in silence, Arnold limited his activity to twiddling his glass, clockwise, anticlockwise and clockwise again, while contemplating the uninteresting spectacle as fixedly as a volunteer for hypnosis. In this somnolent state, he was unable to defend himself against intrusion.

"Do you mind if I sit here?" inquired an ordinary-looking man of average height and width in a dark-grey suit, a white shirt and a silk tie of dark-red and dark-blue stripes. Apparently, he had reached the middle years of his life without having achieved any significant lines in his pale, round face. The only indication of any sort of originality was the arrangement of his meager, black hair, which had been brushed straight forward in the style of Napoleon I; however, that attempt to make the most of little merely revealed vanity.

Arnold looked one way and the other the length of the bar, confirming his early impression of its stretches of emptiness. He wished he had the strength of character to say he did mind the prospect of having this stranger sit immediately next to him; but Arnold lacked the confidence to be deliberately rude, and he felt that the stranger must be desperate for conviviality if he sought such evanescent companionship. Various considerations of this nature passed through Arnold's mind in the second it took to shrug his shoulders in unwelcoming acquiescence.

The stranger ordered a Chivas and Perrier with a twist. This time the bartender offered no congratulations but withdrew right away to do some more unnecessary polishing. Arnold wondered whether his present sense of abject boredom was a sample of moods to come on his travels.

"Staying in the house?" the man asked in the friendliest possible way.

"Only tonight."

"I live in Port Washington, but tonight what the hell."

A blip on the domestic radar, Arnold surmised, without curiosity.

"My name is Lance," the man said, thrusting forward a chubby hand that Arnold was unable to abstain from shaking.

"Arnold. Hi."

That was the best he could do. There was a lapse, while they both sipped their drinks. Arnold actually smiled, looking straight ahead, as he analyzed the incompatibility of the sharp name and its blunt owner.

"What do you do?" Lance wanted to know. The familiar barroom question, if not fended off, could open the way to many more questions.

"Nothing much," Arnold replied. "I came up to have a look at Harlem."

"Harlem! You're going to *Harlem*? Are you out of your mind?"

"Why not Harlem?"

"Why not?" Lance echoed. He laughed, a cynical bark. "It's a jungle up there, that's why not. It's all drugs and guns and knives. You'll be lucky if you're only mugged. They're sex maniacs. AIDS is rife."

"It's what?"

"Rife."

"Rifer than in Port Washington?"

Lance shook his head in disapproval, shocked by Arnold's implication that Harlem and Port Washington were on the same planet.

"Do you know Harlem?" Arnold asked, forgetting his reluctance to engage in dialogue.

"There's no need to go there. Everyone knows what it's like."

"All sex and violence? Sodomy and mayhem?"

"OK, wise guy," Lance said. He gulped the rest of his drink, tossed a bill beside his empty glass, turned and left.

Arnold sighed. After a third and final brandy, he was optimistically sleepy. But when he lay in bed, half asleep, he wondered whether there was any truth in Lance's warning.

19

Arnold travelled uptown in the subway, for the atmosphere. He had expected dimly lighted black and grey stone and metal as grim as a Doré steel engraving for Dante's *Inferno*. However, everything underground had been freshly painted and brilliantly illuminated and the trains were as clean and shiny as new.

He undertook the journey in the Eighth Avenue Express, the most famous train in the world. The Orient Express may rank second. The Eighth Avenue Express is the "A" Train. When Billy "Sweet Pea" Strayhorn wrote "Take the 'A' Train" in 1941, his collaborator Duke Ellington adopted the composition as his theme song. His band played it worldwide, almost every night until he died. The song says

You must take the 'A' Train
To go to Sugar Hill way up in Harlem.

So Arnold took it, but got off a bit before Sugar Hill.

That fine May morning, Harlem did not look at all like a slum. In the sunshine, the boulevards and parks looked like one of the more elegant arrondissements of Paris. Paris, France. Since Peter Stuyvesant, the last Dutch governor of what is now called New York, founded the village of Nieuw Haarlem in 1658, there have been developments, most of them improvements. Now, for example, there is a YMCA.

The Harlem YMCA allowed Arnold a room on the seventh floor of their building, as massive as a fortress, on 135th Street. The young Puerto Rican woman at Reception said she did not know for sure but Room 726 could have been where Langston Hughes lived when his poems were helping to inspire the Harlem Renaissance of the 1920s. Actually, he had lived at the old Y across the street. The big, new one was built in 1932.

In the present era of Harlem's second rebirth, Arnold's assigned place in the Y was exactly the sort of room he liked most of all—monastically austere. It was so small and simple, with a single bed, an unvarnished wooden table and chair and a window overlooking nothing more distracting than rooftops, that it made him feel mentally hygienic. The previous night's morbid fantasy had faded away. He could imagine writing a good book there. If only he could stay....

Anyway, here was another sunny morning. In spite of all the brandy, Arnold felt invigorated. His long sleep had been as perfectly blank as death. He walked briskly westward along 135th, past the Community Democratic Club, picked up *The New York Times*, *The Amsterdam News*, a long-established Harlem weekly, and the May issue of *Ebony* magazine at the corner newsstand, and crossed Adam Clayton Powell Jr Boulevard to a recommended restaurant that served breakfast all day.

A waitress as enormously genial as Scarlett O'Hara's mammy-figure in *Gone With The Wind* handed him a menu and said, "God has sent us a fine day. Enjoy!" The restaurant's place-mat slogan promised a cornucopia. "It's Like Breakfast With Lunch Inside." The menu's first breakfast suggestion, "Colorado Omelette," was said to contain bacon, pork sausage, shredded beef, ham, onions, green peppers and Cheddar cheese. A footnote added that "All omelettes are served with three fluffy buttermilk pancakes." Harlem was securely established in the Land of Plenty.

Arnold settled for orange juice, waffles with hot sauce like liquefied strawberry jam and a dollop of whipped cream, and a quart Thermos of coffee. Drinking coffee and more coffee, he looked through the papers and the magazine.

The *Times* reported everything from everywhere, except, on this occasion, Harlem. *The Amsterdam News* focused on Harlem, and events in the rest of New York City, Albany and Washington that affected Harlem. *Ebony* was devoted nation wide to African-American success stories in industry and commerce, politics, sport and show business. In fact, articles in all three publications could be evaluated and understood best by the criteria of showbiz. The general coverage was state-of-the-art, but Arnold found vestiges of tradition in *The Amsterdam News*'s classified ads. "QUEEN OF OBEAH, Jamaican-born miracle worker," guaranteed immediate results in love and court cases. And an even more remote heritage still resonated: "AFRICAN WITCH DOCTOR, 37 yrs exp," promised the removal of "Demons and Evil Spirits."

At the Schomburg Center for Research in Black Culture, also on 135th Street, Arnold later came across a photograph of a parade of Harlem women in the 1930s bearing banners proclaiming their faith in the man known as Father Divine: "Father Divine is the Supplier and Satisfier of Every Good Desire" and "Father Divine is God Almighty."

The essence of the unusual classified ads and proclamations was not peculiar to Harlem alone. They reminded Arnold of the televised press conferences in the White House.

20

Arnold felt no guilty responsibility for history. But near the corner of 135th Street and Malcolm X Boulevard, still known as Lenox Avenue, there was a graffito, stencilled black on the grey sidewalk, which gave him a twinge of WASP embarrassment. It said:

They stole us
They sold us
Reparations
Now! Now!

How much money could compensate living African Americans for the length of time, more than two hundred years, that their ancestors spent enslaved? Five billion dollars? Fifty billion ? Was any amount enough?

He came to a high steel-mesh fence enclosing an asphalt playground and a mid-morning recess throng of shouting, laughing, happily squealing children playing several simultaneous games of basketball. Along the facade of the school building, a sign proclaimed in large, black capital letters: "HARLEM PLAYS THE BEST BALL IN THE COUNTRY."

He remembered a movie of The Harlem Globetrotters. The children were doing their utmost to justify the claim, which could be applied to every kind of ball game being played by African-Americans in Harlem and beyond, in all of the fifty states. Perhaps, Arnold thought, the professional ball-players were already taking some of what their people believed they had coming to them.

A secretary conducted him from the principal's office to a door in a polished corridor of doors. In a third-grade classroom, a young woman was teaching about thirty children averaging eight years of age at rows of computers on individual desks. Arnold's arrival was an interruption, which the children appeared to be pleased to welcome. The secretary explained to the teacher that he was an author of children's books whom the principal was permitting to audit the lesson. The teacher directed him to a chair beside the blackboard, facing the room.

She told him her name was Lucille Harding and he gave her his.

He guessed she was in her late twenties. She was svelte in a crimson trouser-suit. She had hair as smooth and shiny as black patent leather and the café au-lait complexion of the fashion models in *Ebony*, advertising cosmetics that lighten the color of the skin and the High Definition Power Balm that straightens the hair. She was nearly as beautiful as if she were still black. Her smile revealed perfect teeth.

"Our visitor is Arnold Bosworth," she informed the class. "Mr Bosworth writes books." She turned to him and asked for titles.

"I guess the best-known ones are my stories about Squidgy the Squirrel," he replied with a modest smile, looking around for possible acclamation.

"Oh. Oh, yes," she said. "We used to use them in our class work. I think we still keep them in the library." Turning to her pupils with an encouraging smile, she said: "Hands up everyone who has read a Squidgy book."

Two girls and one boy raised their hands. To Arnold, Lucille said: "Most of the children like DVDs that complement books about 'Star Wars' and other stories about space, anything with plenty of action. You know, life-and-death struggles with aliens and robots and all that."

"My daddy hunted squirrels when we lived in Carolina," a boy in the front row volunteered, as if to console Arnold. "South

Carolina. My mom cooked them in stews." He giggled. "They tasted horrible."

Arnold was trying to think of some up-beat response when the door suddenly burst open and a small boy clattered in—he couldn't have been more than seven—flourishing what appeared to be a blue-steel .45 Magnum. He triumphantly pointed it at Arnold.

"You're dead meat!" the boy shouted. Then he waved the gun from side to side at the whole room. "You're all dead."

Arnold considered leaping at the intruder to disarm him. This was an excellent opportunity to be a hero. Somehow, though, he was unable to move.

Much to his surprise, Lucille's voice was calm and firm.

"Bradford," she said, holding out an authoritative hand, "give me that stupid toy. Your behavior is very anti-social, arriving late, disrupting the class. I'm sure our visitor isn't at all impressed. Please excuse him, Mr Bosworth. He thinks he's funny. Unfortunately, there are shops that sell children these realistic facsimile weapons. Hand it over, Bradford."

"Don't come near me, Miss Harding," the boy warned, stepping back a couple of paces. "I'm not kidding. I'm going to blow his head off. Yours too if you get in the way."

So saying, he squeezed the trigger.

The gun was a real one, with real bullets, as used by Clint Eastwood (Dirty Harry) and other white protectors of law and order. Bradford must have taken it from his father's bedside table or the glove compartment of the family car or from his mother's handbag. His mother always carried a bag large enough to hold a .45.

But nothing happened, because the gun had a safety catch, a device that Bradford had never heard of. Dismayed, he looked at the gun and shook it. When Lucille gently disengaged it from his small hand, he collapsed and sat on the floor, weeping tears of embarrassment, while the class cheered and laughed as uproariously as the studio audience of a sitcom.

21

Lucille Harding was on duty in the school cafeteria at lunchtime that day. She agreed to meet Arnold later, to discuss educational matters that had been put aside by the young gunslinger. Arnold suggested a venue away from the school. Dinner, perhaps? Early? He told her his guidebook recommended Velma's on Lenox Avenue. Lucille said OK.

They ordered the sort of meal that enables white tourists in Harlem to feel they are on a cultural safari, eating the food that black folks are said to eat—shrimp gumbo, fried chicken, collard greens, blackeyed peas, grits and cornbread and other goodies relished down home in Dixie, whereas Velma's family had been at home among Yankees for many decades. Residents of Harlem enjoyed this exotic fare as an occasional change from burgers and french fries. Lucille would have preferred steak, medium rare, and a green salad, but was too polite to say so. She did not want to disillusion her host. Arnold shared her secret preference, but did not want to disillusion his guest. They both made sacrifices for the sake of manifest tolerance.

"I'm sorry about this morning's incident," she said. "Bradford was just showing off. He must have seen you coming from the principal's office. Maybe he had that gun in his locker. We can't check all the lockers all the time. Anyway, in third grade we don't really have a racism problem. That type of demonstration doesn't happen often in our school."

"No, of course not."

"That boy needs counselling, and he shall have it."

"I imagine there are a lot of guns."

"All the families have guns, of course, for their protection. But they normally do their best to prevent their kids from getting their hands on them, and usually they don't succeed in bringing them to school."

"Not many recent massacres."

"I thought you were serious."

"I am," Arnold said. "I was out of line there. But the idea of children and all those—"

"There is hardly any violence in P.S. 132, except for ordinary playground bullying. Some children are bullies. That's an aspect of competition, the free-enterprise ethos. It's human nature."

"Yes."

"Our students are highly motivated by ambition. They're ambitious to become rich and famous."

"Famous for being famous."

"And in a hurry," Lucille said. "I'll give you a for instance. One of our brightest kids, Ella Mae Banville, was moved to the Harlem School of Arts right after First Grade. By her seventh birthday she was a Suzuki Method violinist, playing all the classics on a violin this size." Lucille held her hands not very far apart. "I mean, she was *good.* Mozart is nice, but her mother had bigger goals. She entered Ella Mae into Amateur Night at the Apollo. She won the top spot playing and singing a rap song of her own composition. Instant recording contract! They say she's already heading for her first gold disc. You know what I'm saying?"

"Phenomenal!"

"That's not a unique case. To sum up, black children are the same as white children, except that black children are black."

Arnold telephoned Naomi Swartkop next morning. "I'm afraid Harlem has been a waste of time," he said. "The children there all want to be pop stars, star actors and star models, star ball-players and star TV personalities. In other words, they're like everybody else, all over the country."

"Great," Naomi said. "Homogeneity means efficient marketing. You're off to a fine start."

22

Meanwhile, back in Annapolis, on the playground of John Paul Jones Elementary, Angelica's best friend, always ahead when it came to affairs of the heart, continued her campaign against human heterosexuality.

"Men and women do it like animals," Bobo said. "The woman's on her hands and knees, and the man pushes himself into her from behind, like a dog. Or a pig. Eeyuck!"

"But I thought—"

"Yeah, I know. Sometimes the man lies on top and they can look in each other's faces while they're doing it. That's called the missionary position, because missionaries told people they were converting in tropical countries that that was the only way God wanted people to fuck. But usually people do it like animals. If you don't believe me, watch 'Naughty Girls' on adult TV. I've seen 'Naughty Girls in Vegas,' 'Naughty Girls in Paris' and 'Naughty Girls in Tokyo'—they're all the same. They go at it like animals. Have a look for yourself. It's an on-going series of genuine documentaries, not fiction." Bobo gave Angelica the channel and the time. "When you watch those animals—those people—think of your darling daddy doing it to your darling stepmother."

"Don't be so horrible!" Angelica said, her pretty blue eyes glittering with tears. She could not help remembering the sight and sounds of two fugitive Rottweilers copulating in urgent spasms, right there on the antique brick sidewalk of the Bosworths' National Heritage street. The dog at the back was snarling and the bitch in front was panting with her tongue hanging out.

"My daddy's not like other people," Angelica said.

"How do you think you got to be born?" Bobo demanded with a sarcastic grin. "Did a guy in a lab mix up some magic in a glass dish? Come on, Angie, get real! Daddy must have done it to your mom, and now he must do it to that new woman. But you'll have options. You don't want some creep with a shaved head and a skin problem to stick his thing into you, do you? Do you know what it's like, having a baby? My mom says it's like shitting a basketball."

Bobo's way with words made Angelica queasy, but also made her do some earnest thinking.

In her bedroom late that evening, after the fun-for-the-family romantic soaps and horror movies, Angelica locked the door. Her zapper quickly found "Naughty Girls in Waikiki," in the throes of an orgy.

Bobo had not exaggerated. Angelica was appalled and fascinated. Was she destined to look like the women on the screen when she grew up? Would she have huge, round silicone breasts with rigid, dark nipples, and pubic hair trimmed like a topiary bush? Would she be expected to massage, fondle and kiss giants with the bulging muscles and limited vocabularies of Mr Universes? The Naughty Girls twisted and turned this way and that (and even that!), bumping and grinding, like Rubens models on amphetamines, and the moronic weightlifters compliantly did their utmost to move reciprocally in time, yet not to come. Angelica flinched as she seemed to see her father's face and Cynthia's superimposed on those of the playgirls.

There had to be some way of stopping him. There just had to be.

Angelica did not want to watch any more, but she remained on the edge of her bed, staring as though hypnotized by the welter of gleaming bodies, when there was a loud banging at the door.

She agitatedly stumbled to the door and spoke close to the varnished pine.

"Yes?"

The banging continued for a while, then Cynthia replied.

"I can hear what's going on. Unlock this door at once!"

"What do you want?"

The banging started again, faster and louder. Angelica obeyed.

Cynthia pushed the door open, pushing Angelica aside.

The Naughty Girls were still writhing about with their naughty companions.

"Filth!" Cynthia screamed in a smoky, phlegmy voice hoarse after an evening of the Ersdales' hospitality. "You disgusting, disgusting, dis-*gusting* little bitch!"

The almost-36-year-old woman slapped the face of the 9-year-old girl so hard that she staggered sideways several feet across the bedroom, a hand pressed against her hot cheek.

"You're as bad as your goddamned father!" Cynthia added. She strode to the television and yanked the plug from the wall. As if that might not be enough censorship, she ripped the black, rubber-covered lead from the back of the set and flung it to the floor.

Angelica did not move or speak. She watched Cynthia's back as she stormed from the room and slammed the door.

Angelica went down to the kitchen at the usual time next day. Cynthia was in bed.

Angelica had almost finished her Sugar Pops when her stepmother arrived to make some coffee.

"Angie—"

"My name is Angelica. Only Daddy and my best friend call me Angie."

"We can't go on like this," Cynthia said. Her manner was carefully controlled. "Your behavior may not be entirely your fault. I realize there are harmful influences at the public school you've been attending. And, of course, since your mother passed on, your father has been over-indulging you."

The thought of Arnold's blatant favoritism and all the sickening baby talk caused Cynthia to lose for a moment quite a high percentage of her cool. She coughed and swallowed and made a noticeable effort to stand taller·

"When your father returns," she said, "we're going to arrange for a transfer. I've learned the name of a school in Vermont of great social status. I understand there are ponies. I'm sure I'll be able to convince your father that your education and your general upbringing in all its aspects will benefit from the discipline of a traditional boarding school."

Cynthia permitted herself to smile at her horrified step-daughter. The smile was of the sort that may be classified most charitably as inscrutable.

"A boarding school will be best for you," Cynthia concluded. "The best for all of us."

On the way to J.P.J., walking alone, Angelica called the St Regis on her mobile. The clerk at reception said Mr Bosworth had checked out. No, he did not leave a forwarding address.

23

The flight from New York was an ordinary twenty-first-century journey. It could have been from anywhere to anywhere else. At JFK, he took off his shoes to show they did not contain explosives.

He walked slowly through an archway metal-detector, and was thoroughly frisked. He was allowed to pick up his briefcase after its examination by x-ray. Thus reminded again of enemies who wanted to kill him, he settled in his allotted seat aboard the plane and fastened his seat-belt, surrendering himself to forces beyond his control, including gravity and a First Pilot who could be some sort of addict about to suffer at high altitude his first and last incapacitating nervous seizure.

"Travelling for business or pleasure?" inquired the man in the next seat.

"Yes," Arnold said. "I mean, I hope so. A little of each."

The friendly interrogation was terminated by an announcement demanding his attention to a briefing on procedures that might save his life in an emergency. Attached to the inflatable yellow lifejacket, there was a whistle for attracting rescuers.

After taxiing for a mile or two, the plane turned on to a runway and moved forward with a sudden surge of power. As always, Arnold devoutly wished they would accelerate fast enough to get off the ground before the runway ended.

As always up till then, they did so, and his entrails unknotted.

Kansas City is bipartite. The western part of the city is in Kansas; the eastern part is in Missouri. At the KC airport, which is in Missouri, Arnold was advised to stay in Missouri.

"It's where the action is," said the woman at Information. "You know, the best designer boutiques, the best barbecues, the best jazz, the best casino. Missouri invented the ice-cream cone, the hot dog and iced tea. Kansas City, Missouri, is where you'll find the world-famous, historic Country Club Plaza. It has more fountains than any other city but Rome."

"All I need is the name of a hotel," he said.

"The best accommodation is in the Plaza," she promised. She

recited the names of several hotels in chains of international repute. He knew they maintained the same standard of quality control in identical establishments from Reykjavik to Macau, so, trying to play safe, he picked one of the familiar brand names. His trip to the geographic center of the United States would be for its symbolic significance; he would sleep in Missouri. He phoned for a room and rented a car.

Prohibition was the happy time in Kansas City. When Tom Prendergast was boss, until spoilsports indicted him for tax evasion, the city was wide open. Bootleg liquor flowed like Niagara night and day, and the sounds of jazz were heard in every brothel. At that time, it was the nation's best jazz. Count Basie took it from KC to New York, and radio spread it from coast to coast.

However, Kansas City seemed relatively tame by the time Arnold arrived. The Country Club was a retail shopping theme park, with enough terracotta, floral tiles, mosaic and fountains for a Spanish Disneyland. It was all so modern, bright and clean! There wasn't a hint of sex and violence.

The lobby of the Hotel Seville Ritz-Plaza was as lofty and hushed as a cathedral. A Mexican wearing a clip-on maroon bow tie and blazer consulted a computer and confirmed that Arnold was permitted to stay. He pressed a button for an elevator and there was an almost immediate *ping*, and in a few seconds he was on the nineteenth floor. After walking along a silent corridor the length of a football field, he was soon able to insert and withdraw the electronic card that opened his door. Having waived a uniformed porter's assistance (he hated paying someone to show him that the bathroom was a bathroom and the television set was a television set), he carried in his suitcase and looked around for the mini-bar. He had travelled half-way across the country and was in a bedroom very much like the one he had occupied at the St Regis, but somewhat smaller.

He removed his jacket and tie, washed his hands and face, mixed a gin and tonic, sat in an armchair and looked through visitors' guides. The biggest advertisements were for casinos. One of them typically offered "More casino. More fun," with 2,900 slot machines and a creche at hourly rates, "where your kids will have fun so you can too!" Like distillers and brewers who advise drinkers to enjoy drinks "sensibly," the casinos expressed tender-hearted concern that gamblers should not let gambling harm them.

"Know when to stop before you start," one casino advised at the foot of its ad, in microscopic type. "Gambling problem? Call 1-888-BETSOFF." How much more considerate than the card-sharps of the Mississippi riverboats and the saloons of the Old West! Before long, Arnold imagined, the new impresarios, ever mindful of the importance of harmonious public relations, would provide broke gamblers with psychiatric therapy on the house and free rides home.

He read in brochures about the Plaza's rich profusion of ethnic eateries—McCormick & Schmick's Seafood, P. F. Chang's China Bistro, Brio Tuscan Grille, Hibachi Japanese Steakhouse, Mi Cocina Restaurant Mexicana, O'Dowd's Little Dublin and Topsy's Popcorn Shoppe and many more. So many that he lost his appetite and decided to stay in his room. The armchair was comfortable. He got another bottle of Beefeater from the mini-bar.

He was complacently dozing when there was a demanding *rat-a-tat-tat* at the door.

"Yes?" he asked cautiously, opening the door a few inches.

"Room service!" The voice was a young girl's.

"I didn't order anything," he said, opening the door all the way. There was only a girl standing out there. She was about the same age as Angelica, with the same Alice-in-Wonderland blonde hair and blue eyes, and wearing a white T-shirt and blue jeans.

"You don't look like room service," he said.

She grinned.

"You don't seem to be carrying a tray," he went on, the whimsical, avuncular writer of children's books. "I don't see any sign of a trolley. Anyway, you have come to the wrong room. Who are you looking for?"

She had a sweet face and he did not mean to give an impression of severity.

"You may use the phone to get things straightened out, if you wish," he offered with a kindly smile, leaning down a little from his superior height.

"I give special room service. You're Mr Bosworth, right? I saw you when you arrived. Sometimes I sit in the lobby, checking people out. You look nice. I got your room number from the desk. My name's Marcia. I can explain. Can I come in?"

"I suppose so. For a minute. I have work to do."

He moved aside. She smiled and entered the room.

"Well?" he said.

He was still near the open door, holding the inside knob.

"I can make you feel really fantastic," she said. "I mean like really. At school, even the seniors say I'm the best. It's only twenty-five dollars."

"What on earth are you talking about? Shouldn't you be heading home by now? Don't you have homework to do?"

"I need the money. I'm saving up for theater school. I've already signed for evening classes this fall. Twenty-five dollars isn't a big deal for you. I guarantee I'm worth it."

"You look too young to be selling drugs, Marcia, if that's what you're trying to do." Arnold managed to utter a good-natured chuckle.

His facetiousness made her frown. With dignity, she said: "The boys call me 'Miss Blow Job.'"

"That isn't funny. You shouldn't talk like that."

"Who said anything about funny?"

"You'd better leave."

"If you don't want it, just pay me. Or how would you feel if I started screaming? That'd make you look kinda silly, wouldn't it?"

"Please, Marcia. You must go. Now."

She remained in the middle of the room. Instead of screaming, she took a mobile phone from her hip pocket and nimbly fingered some numbers.

"What are you doing?" he demanded uneasily. Was the girl mad?

To the phone, she said: " Help—and fast!" To Arnold, she said: "He'll be right up."

Arnold asked who "he" was, but she ignored the question. It was answered soon enough. A thickset man of middle age burst in as if responding to a fire alarm. He had a shaven head shiny with sweat and a thick face that looked like that of an unsuccessful prizefighter in resentful retirement. The tightness of his black suit was threatening.

"What do *you* want?" Arnold asked.

"Security," the man announced, taking some sort of laminated card from inside his jacket and flashing it so fast it could have been a driving license or extraterrestrial credentials from a cereal packet. Or authentic ID. "There ain't no call to come on in that tone of voice. I know your type. I bet you're from back east." He turned to the girl. "What happened, child?"

"He told me he had a wonderful gift for me," the girl said. "But as soon as we came up to his room he unzipped his pants and—"

"That's a lie!" Arnold protested. "Marcia, you know that isn't true."

"My name isn't Marcia."

"A nut case," commented the house detective or whatever he was. "We have laws in Kansas City. Maybe you can get away with this kind of behavior where you come from, buddy, but here we throw the book at child-molesters. If I called the KCPD to send assistance you'd be in deep shit. Her word against yours. But maybe we can work something out."

"How did she know your mobile number?"

"Marylouise is the daughter of a very distinguished Kansas Citizen. You wouldn't want to cross him. He's big in the Elks. His family are respected patrons of the Ritz-Plaza. Naturally she's been given my number for emergencies. The best thing you can do is settle, and we'll be able to forget the whole thing. You're lucky. I'm in a good mood and I hate paper-work. I'm giving you a break."

Arnold thought of Naomi Swartkop. He thought of Cynthia. Worst of all, he thought of Angelica. The situation was grossly unfair. The scandal, seen from a distance, would look terrible. Who would believe him? He felt himself weaken.

"I don't think I have even twenty-five dollars on me," he said. "I'm planning to use my hotel account and go to the bank in the morning." He fished some bills from a trouser pocket, two tens and three ones. "Look."

"You have credit cards, don't you?"

Arnold nodded.

"Good, because the price has gone up to five hundred dollars. There's a cash machine on the ground floor."

"This is ridiculous!" Arnold protested.

"That's what pedophiles always say," commented the protector of security. "A lawyer would cost a lot more, believe me, plus a huge fine—only a fine if he was real sharp."

Nobody spoke in the elevator.

After Arnold handed over the pile of crisp, new twenty-dollar bills, the big man and the small girl walked together across the lobby, away from him.

As they pushed their way through the revolving door, Arnold heard their hoots of laughter.

24

Arnold got up at dawn. His recollection of the previous afternoon was like a bad dream. He wanted fresh air and plenty of it. Kansas is good for that. He made an early start for a long drive. Be drove northward to St Joseph, Missouri, and westward through Troy, Kansas; Hiawatha and Fairview, and, at last, through Lebanon to the geographic center of the United States. He parked the car and walked to Center Park, at 39.81 degrees North, 98.55 West. The government geodetic surveyors of 1898 had calculated the coordinates to ten decimal places, so he knew for sure exactly where he was.

He stood at the heart of the American heartland and contemplated the stone structure that marks the spot. The small, truncated pyramid resembles the one on the cryptic reverse side of the Great Seal of the United States, as depicted on the dollar bill. There, on the bill, a single Masonic eye in a radiant nimbus counterbalances the thirteen stars above the eagle clutching a thirteen-leaf olive branch in one set of claws and a sheaf of thirteen arrows in the other. Right from the start, America has always offered peace or else.... He felt uplifted by a patriotic epiphany that transcended blackmail and the demands of his commercial mission for Varoom! Children's Books. He was a free, independent, original American author seeking the essential spirit of American children's aspirations. Yesterday had been horrible; before him now he seemed to visualize the ideal, the real thing. In his mind, he heard the echo of some words of Walter Scott's that he had been assigned at school at the age of eight, when he was expected to memorize poetry at home and recite bits of it in class.

Scott had written:

Breathes there the man, with soul so dead,
Who never to himself hath said,
This is my own, my native land!

Some of the best Americans were of Scottish descent. Though Arnold's birthplace was in Maryland, near the small-scale charms of Annapolis, he recognized in Kansas the ultimate grand sweep of Americanness. He felt a frisson of pride that ancestral pioneers had conquered, occupied and cultivated this vast land. He regarded the declining amber rays of the sun westering over the loneliness of the prairie, the distant horizon beneath the immense sky, and believed that he stood at the very quintessence of tradition, on the threshold of a glorious literary future. Here he was in the place that well-brought-up, right-thinking children loved best of all, The Land of Oz. Surely, he thought, he had crossed over the rainbow.

In a ruminant trance, he reminisced about Dorothy and her beloved dog Toto, the magical cyclonic whirlwind, the benign Witch of the North, the grateful liberated Munchkins and Dorothy's companions, the straw Scarecrow who yearned for a brain, the Tin Woodman who yearned for a heart and the Cowardly Lion who yearned for bravery, who all walked with her along the yellow-brick road to the Emerald City, to the Wizard himself, who was called wonderful even though he was a fraud. He was a little man with P.T. Barnum's grandiose gift of the gab, who hid behind a big screen in his palace, ruled Oz by ventriloquism and illusion, and was able to give the Scarecrow, the Tin Woodman and the Cowardly Lion everything they wanted, and eventually to waft Dorothy and Toto home again, only because they believed that he could. How Madison Avenue! How Hollywood!

These nostalgic philosophical notions were abruptly interrupted by the babble and laughter of a gang of children on a cultural expedition from Kansas City. Having finished their picnic on the far side of the Center, they were on their way to the yellow school bus to begin the long return trip. Arnold saw that the boys and girls were about the ages of those Naomi classified as his "target readership," bless them!, so he took the opportunity to accost one of them. He stopped a boy wearing a black Stetson, a Harrah's Casino T-shirt, blue jeans and black boots.

"No school today?" Arnold asked in the bright adult-to-child way that tends to widen the generation gap.

"This is a school project."

"Oh, of course. The geographic center. It reminds me of Oz. Have you read *The Wonderful Wizard of Oz*?"

The boy looked quizzical, expressing both scorn and pity. After a withering pause, he said:

"Crapola."

"What?"

"That book's a bunch of crap," the boy explained, extending the comment for the sake of clarity.

Arnold was taken aback.

"But it's everyone's favorite story in the whole of America, isn't it?" he said. "It's been Number One for more than a hundred years."

"Kids don't buy it. Their moms do. Miss Collins says the guy who wrote it was a total dweeb."

"Did I hear my name?" queried a young redhead in big purple sunglasses, a Potawatomi Nation T-shirt and a silver and turquoise necklace. "Not in vain, I hope." She submitted Arnold to a quick once over and apparently approved sufficiently to linger for a while. "Is our Leroy, the scourge of the Fourth Grade, bothering you?"

"No, not at all," Arnold assured her with a conciliatory smile. "I was remembering the Wizard of Oz, and wondered what he thought o£ the book, and he told me. I'm interested in children's books. I'm doing a survey. As an elementary-school teacher, you may have heard of me. My name is Arnold Bosworth."

Miss Collins smiled.

"I'm afraid not," she said. "But I admit I'm not an expert on every author. There are thousands of them, aren't there?"

"Don't you know the stories of Squidgy the Squirrel?" In his voice there was a slight quiver of pathos.

Leroy shrugged his little shoulders, grinned and winked up at the teacher. She gave him a brief frown to request restraint.

"Sorry," she said to Arnold. "I majored in Computer Science and this is my first year teaching. Anyway, I can quickly look up anything I need to know. I'll Google you when we get back. Speaking of getting back, I see my flock is becoming restive. We're setting up tents for an overnight break half-way and they like that."

"You didn't call the author of the Oz books a total dweeb, did you?" Arnold persisted.

She laughed.

"Those aren't my words, but they're quite good ones to sum up what I think. I told the class L. Frank Baum was a racist. When he owned a newspaper in South Dakota, he wrote an editorial advocating extermination of all Indians, as they used to be called—all Native Americans—because he suspected they were plotting revenge for the massacre at Wounded Knee. Custer's regiment could never forget what the Indians did to them at Little Big Horn. If Baum were editorializing today he'd call them terrorists."

"But must you let a writer's private life, his political opinions, his social behavior, his—"

"Sure I must. I know what you're on about," she said in a teacherly, soothing manner. "It's an interesting question. Should we honor fiction by suicidal addicts and fascist beasts? I don't have time for that discussion right now. We have to be on our way. If you're going to spend some time in KC, why don't you visit with us? The class would value your input. Me too. Possibly you and I would enjoy coffee and a chat."

"Great!"

She wrote the school's name and location and telephone number and e-mail address in his notebook. Arnold felt hard-wired.

As she and the children hurried away along a path through the neat plantation of shrubbery and trees, he watched the rolling side-to-side swaying of her hips. The blue denim of her jeans hugged her tight.

It was a shame, he thought, that she, like almost every child, had such a fat ass.

25

Miss Collins' Fourth-Graders at Kate Smith Elementary took a twenty-minute refreshment break at 10.30 a.m. every school day. "It gives the kids' blood sugar a needed boost for optimum concentration during the final session before lunch," she told Arnold, as she led him from her classroom to the fluorescently lighted, pale-peach and stainless-steel cafeteria. "We're proud of our cafeteria. Our menus are the envy of the whole school district."

Sidling along the self-service counter with his pale-peach plastic tray, he was able to hear the comments and debates of the boys and girls making their selections behind their teacher and himself.

"The new mammoth shakes are bigger!"

"Yeah, sure, but the jumbos are thicker, and there's more added flavoring."

"They put more antacids in the mammoths."

"So have mammoth. Me, I'll stay with jumbo."

The disagreements were emotionally intense but reasonable.

"They're knowledgeable, appreciative and critical of the diet provided by the catering franchisees," Miss Collins said. "The kids are very product-aware. The TV commercials at home inculcate super-sophistication foodwise, from First Grade on up. The kids know all the leading brand names, the nutritional values of the various pizza toppings and fruit sodas and everything. They know what they want, and they get it."

After hardly any hesitation, she opted for butterscotch cream from the array of 45-degree segments of pies.

"I really recommend this," she said. "It's one of my favorites. And don't worry: the butterscotch is low-cal."

"That's quite a display of pastries and cakes," he said politely. He chuckled. "And the size of the donuts!"

"Take a couple. Do. The jam ones are extra energizing. After the break, the kids do some of their most creative programming."

"Everything looks very good, but thanks, I'll just have a coffee." She looked disappointed. Gluttons prefer not to eat alone. "I had a big breakfast," he apologetically explained.

"Well, make it a cappuccino. It's slim-line."

He complied. White froth hissed from the chrome-plated cappuccino machine at the same time as another machine finished agitating her mocha malted.

She guided him to a table only big enough for two. A bud vase in the middle of it contained a single white plastic rosebud. An overhead spotlight brightened the highlights of her auburn curls, but had an unflattering effect on her pretty face. Though obviously still so young, the fine features were already blurring in lines no longer slim. When she laughed, as she did when settling down to her pie with the enthusiasm of young womanhood, her double chin sagged into the soft shapelessness of her neck. Arnold involuntarily imagined a time, in the not very distant future, when increasing puffiness around her brown eyes would cause them to seem to sink like raisins in raw dough. The momentary vision saddened him.

"Don't you like the coffee?" she asked, misinterpreting his expression.

"It's fine. It's still very hot."

"I Googled you and your work," she assured him, "as I said I would."

"Oh?"

"I didn't learn a whole lot about the story of your life."

"There isn't really all that much to tell," he said with a modest smile. "We writers usually have rather boring lives, if we aren't a Hemingway or Hunter S. Thompson or someone like that."

"But at least Google gave me the titles of your books. There've been a lot of them, haven't there?"

"Just about enough to keep the wolf from the door."

"I found a couple of them in our library, back in the stacks. I hate to tell you but the stamps indicated that recently they haven't been circulating much."

He winced.

"May I call you Arnold?" she asked with a winsome dimpling of her plump cheeks.

"Certainly."

"I'm Lucinda. May I speak frankly?"

"Of course," he replied apprehensively, for nothing encouraging ever follows that request.

"As you must realize, communication these days is almost instantaneous. We zap data exponentially. Like zing."

He nodded earnestly, to signify that he had indeed noticed a general speeding up of things.

"When I looked through a couple of your stories," she said, "I doubted you have been allowing for how fast today's children process the impressions that continually hit on them. Facts and factoids in megabytes."

"I'm not quite sure what you mean," Arnold admitted.

"What I'm trying to tell you, without hurting your feelings, is that reading is the slowest way of assimilating material, and kids have no patience for stories in written words unless they come close to the pace of moving pictures. Did you ever see the Maigret movies on TV by the great French writer Simian?"

"Simenon. Georges Simenon. He was Belgian. Why?"

With a backhand wave, Lucinda dismissed her inaccuracies as irrelevant.

"OK, Simenon. Whatever. According to an article about him in *Teacher's Digest*, he could write one of his Maigret novels in seven days. You know how?"

"No. I've wondered how."

"He cut right to the chase. No waste. He said he limited his vocabulary to two thousand easy words, so no one would have to go to the dictionary. Your books are too slow, Arnold. There are too many descriptions, too much about what people are feeling and thinking, too many words, too much punctuation.

"Kids don't give a shit—pardon my French!—about the colors of a sunset. They only want to know what happens next and next and next."

She reminded him of Naomi Swartkop. Lucinda made him feel

like a dinosaur watching a pterodactyl fly, jealous and resentful. Arnold could tell her and her wonderful children a thing or two.

26

In the classroom before the break, Arnold had been as silent as wallpaper. Now, Lucinda having urged him to share his impressions with the class, he felt free to assert himself. Her comments on his work had hurt.

"Frankly," he said, using the teacher's supposedly disarming way of introducing negative criticism, "when I accepted Miss Collins's invitation to visit your fine school and get to know you boys and girls, I came here expecting only to exchange our thoughts about literature. But I would be remiss if I didn't tell you what I believe are even more important problems than that of deciding which books you should read.

"Let me give it to you straight," he continued, galvanized by righteous zeal. "Your computer Spel-Cheks can correct your text-message-type misspellings; however, computers can't think for you. You have to think in your minds, in language you know. To think logically and creatively, you need verbal clarity. You need to understand syntax, grammar, the interconnections of words. To achieve poetry, Coleridge said, you have to arrange 'the best words in the best order.'" Arnold was only subliminally aware that his audience was becoming restless. "But that isn't the most urgent matter of all.

"I have a daughter about your age. Her name is Angelica. She and her best girlfriend recently decided to get rid of their puppy fat. That phrase sounds kind of cute, doesn't it? But the actuality isn't cute at all. Sometimes political correctness, which is neither political nor correct, gets in the way of the truth.

"Whatever you call being fat, being big or heavy or having

surplus avoirdupois, fat is fat. Everyone knows what it is. Fat is a symptom of greed and laziness. It's a warning of future ill health and early death. Look around this room. Look at each other. Most of you are *fat*.

"You eat too much of the wrong food, drink too much of the wrong drink and don't take enough exercise. How many of you walk or bicycle to school? How many hours a day do you sit watching television? Playing virtual-reality games or staring at ball games played for you by professional athletes doesn't keep you in good shape. In fact, most of you are in terrible shape.

"Some other schools have switched to health foods and drinks. I don't know how much good I can do but I'm willing to write to your superintendent to tell of the faults I've observed at Kate Smith Elementary. Or I could try to persuade a local editor to campaign on your behalf. *The Kansas City Star* has a proud tradition of campaigning for worthy causes."

Arnold sighed. There was a general fidgeting in the class, a rising murmur of discontent, a hostile grumbling.

"Thank you, Mr Bosworth," Miss Collins said, rubbing an eyelid with an agitated forefinger. "I think you have said enough. More than enough. Because some people are … big doesn't mean they are insensitive. Anyway, whatever. I can offer you a lift back to your hotel. A school driver can take you. Where are you staying. The Marriott?"

"I'm at the Ritz-Plaza. Thanks, but I have my own car."

He realized he had not been very tactful. "I didn't mean to offend anyone," he said. "I thought it might help if—"

"I'm afraid you have offended just about everyone," she interrupted him. "Deeply."

He apologetically waved goodbye to the children. None of them waved back.

During a solitary lunch in an Italian bistro (lobster soup, a salad and an espresso), he admitted to himself that he had gone too far. The children were not to blame for their lifestyle and condition. Why in most families these days did both parents feel compelled to have jobs that took them away from home all day? Did they really need second mortgages, such extravagant vacations, so many designer labels?

He visited the Toy Museum and an art museum displaying Thomas Hart Benton paintings of Midwestern pioneers with big hands and feet. He mooched about in a bookshop featuring the ghostwritten autobiographies of celebrities of TV, pop music, sports and the garment industry. In the small Children's Department, on the second floor, the latest edition of *The Wonderful Wizard of Oz* was profligately enhanced with illustrations that popped up three-dimensionally when pages were turned, apparently so children would be tempted through the text, with the possibility of reading some of it.

How could he expect to buck the trend? Should he write a letter of apology to Lucinda Collins? She was obviously sensitive about her own image. Her fat.

Oh, shit! he lamented. Furthermore, he lamented that that unlovely but succinctly eloquent Anglo-Saxonism most aptly summarized his perception of contemporary civilization. He might as well return to his hotel, to his bedroom, to the narcosis of the mini-bar and television. On one of the channels, perhaps, if he were lucky, they might be showing an old-fashioned he-man Western.

But he was not that lucky. He was prevented from attaining a comfortable escape when, as the saying goes, the shit hit the fan.

27

"Oh, Mr Bosworth! Thank goodness you're back!" Outside the

main entrance to his hotel, a young tow-headed girl, one of the clinically obese of the Kate Smith fourth-graders, looked up at Arnold with yearning big brown eyes. Her pretty features were not quite totally submerged in the fleshy accretions of countless hundreds of maxiburgers, maxipizzas and humongous cartons of French fries. She was the very personification of a childhood of junk takeaways. Dimples indicated the sites of knuckles in the plump hand that clutched his sleeve. It would have been difficult for anyone to imagine that within the tight blue denim of her jacket and jeans, deep inside the preposterous bulges of her torso and hips and the roly-poly cylinders of her arms and legs, lurked the skeleton of a 9-year-old.

"What is it?" he asked warily. The children's expressions of hatred as he left the classroom were unforgettable.

"Me and my friend came to get your autograph," the child said in an appealing lisp, immediately causing his defenses to crumble.

"You did? And you've been waiting here ever since school got out?"

"In the hotel, they told us you weren't there yet, so we waited outside."

"Sorry," be said, with sincere regret. "Where's your friend? Did he get tired of waiting?"

"She. No, she didn't. I need your help. I think something real horrible's happening to her. This old guy talked her into going with him into the alley. She wouldn't listen to me. I don't know what he promised her, but I heard her scream."

He saw the alley, a narrow entry for deliveries and employees between the hotel and its annex.

"Haven't you raised the alarm? Someone ought to call for the police."

"I don't want a big hassle. You know how the media would

blow it up. She's only been in there a few minutes. With you here, I figure maybe we should go in after her. Maybe that would be enough to stop what's coming down." She frowned. "There's sex crimes. But you'll help us, won't you?" The corrugations of anxiety cleared from her little forehead. Her look of trust showed she depended on him. He must act. Without another word, he hurried to the alley, with her in close pursuit.

Arnold saw no old guy, no young victim, only a red, white and blue Esso tanker, which was almost as wide as the space between the concrete walls.

"They must be further in," the girl said, urging him on.

The ambush was tumultuous and overwhelming. Just beyond the tanker, he was beaten over the head, punched from all sides as he fell, and kicked as he lay dazed and bleeding on a rainbow puddle of oil.

He had fallen foul of the Madonna Gang (named after the pop star rather than the mother of Jesus), the most militant fatties of the fourth grade.

"Give it to him good!" commanded the girl who had got Arnold there. She was the leader.

"That's it! Kick him where it hurts! Let the rotten son of a bitch know what we think of him and his bullshit ideas."

The gang, expert practitioners of the martial arts, required no further instruction. Arnold suffered a fearful pummelling. The girls' small fists felt as hard as rocks.

Their trainers thudded agonizingly into the vital regions of his kidneys and heart. He writhed from side to side, attempting to evade the storm of blows, in vain. At last, he collapsed on his back, holding up his hands in surrender; but the girls were merciless. Encircling him, they lowered their fat faces close, savoring the intimacy of torturers with the tortured. They gloated over him as they replicated some of the entertainment they had witnessed in years of television news, documentaries and dramas, years of thrilling violence in sporting arenas, bedrooms and genocidal massacres all over the world. There was no interrogation of prisoners or marital tiff too brutal for the Madonna Gang's copycat appreciation.

Arnold passed out for a while. A return to semi-consciousness in the pale blue of early dusk was painful. He ached all over. He squinted up at the single light over the door to the hotel kitchen. He perceived everything in hazy duplicate. He wondered how private eyes, when savagely beaten up in movies, never seemed to feel this bad. He shut his eyes, enclosing the pain in the inescapable privacy of his skull.

The next time he came to, he heard the voices of two male paramedics.

"A drunk?"

"I'd say mugged. Look at the abrasions and contusions. Could be the person who phoned in was the person who did it. Guilty conscience? Hotels hire all kinds of foreigners these days. You never know what they're thinking."

"There's a pulse. Do you think he needs mouth-to-mouth?"

"Then you do it. I'm not in the mood, thank you very much."

"His face is a mess."

"Let Casualty fix him up. And let's get going. I was meant to be off at six."

28

"He did a beautiful job," an intern said, delicately fingering Arnold's nose. "Fortunately, Dr D'Alesandro was still here when they brought you in. Our Dr D'Alesandro is the most distinguished nose man in the whole Midwest. Usually he delegates. I guess something about your case must've challenged him. Thanks to him, your nose will soon be almost as good as new. Hardly anyone will ever know how badly it was broken. How was it broken?"

The young apprentice evidently labored under the common delusion that all patients relish chit-chat about their afflictions.

"Aw ahrr" was Arnold's only response. It hurt to open his bruised jaws and hurt to speak between his bruised lips. He was bruised from head to foot. The slightest movement hurt, though he was propped up on soft pillows on an adjustable designer bed in a fragrant private room. His medical insurance policy entitled him to the best accommodation and the best, delay-free investigative examination, physical treatment and around the clock psychological comforting that money could buy, within the guidelines of the American Medical Association, the Hippocratic oath and the *Reader's Digest*.

The hospital was secular; however, should a client, despite the most skillfully administered pharmacology, appear to be about to pass on, spiritual consolation could be provided for him or her and/or the next of kin by a fully qualified minister of any faith of choice, for a reasonable honorarium.

On the first morning of his stay, technicians subjected Arnold to in-depth scrutiny with all the sophisticated apparatus of modern medical science. For example, he was strapped supine in an aluminum and glass tube and inserted head-first into a machine that scanned and calibrated the functions of his innermost organs. Analysis indicated that his pythagoras gland, of which he had been previously unaware, would probably continue to give adequate service for quite some time, if not neutralized by carbohydrates, amino acids and the wrong kind of spring water.

By means of feeble gestures, he asked for, and was given, a notepad and pen.

"Why so many tests?" he scribbled.

"In case of litigation," one of the medical team informed him, but did not suggest who might sue whom, and he was still too dizzy to pursue the question.

On the second day, a nurse escorted a man into Arnold's room who looked like Central Casting's notion of a successful bookie—sleek black hair, smooth red complexion, Fauvist abstract-pattern tie, suit of black silk-mohair and black alligator loafers. Except for the tie, he reminded Arnold of Ersdale, who usually wore dignified British regimentals.

How was Elwood doing? Arnold wondered. How would his own family react when notified of his hospitalization? And Naomi? Would he be blamed? He was not impatient to learn the answers. Anyway, the visitor gave Arnold no time for speculation.

"Hi there, Mr Bosworth," the man said with a cheery smile. "I represent Mahony, Kronerstern and Quark, attorneys at law. I'm Terry Quark, at your service."

"I haven't asked for a lawyer," Arnold objected in a hoarse whisper. He had recently promulgated an up-to-date will in Annapolis, in Cynthia's favor, with Angelica as the sole residual legatee, not that he expected to die right away.

"You are Arnold Bosworth, aren't you? We understand you were the victim of a major assault, resulting in concussion and other damages to your person. Our speciality is settling personal injury claims, on a no-win, no-fee basis."

"How do you know about me?"

"We keep tabs on hospital admissions in the KC area for incidents of potential interest. We have contacts. We can get you a very nice compensation. I'm talking fifty, sixty grand and up. We have a high percentage success rate. Your face looks like a sure thing. Are there any other bad bruises?"

"All over."

"Good. So you're suffering from post-traumatic stress disorder, including loss of libido and professional earning power, right? We'll take photos before the bruises fade. Were there witnesses? Who was the guy that did this to you? Do you know? "

"I know who it was. It wasn't a guy. It was a bunch of kids, about half the four grade of Kate Smith Elementary."

Quark was disappointed, even a bit reproachful.

"Then my trip's a waste of time," he said. "We can't touch kids. They can do anything they like."

Near the door, he paused, turned back and said, lowering his voice: "We also handle medical negligence and malpractice. Do you have any grievances along those lines?"

But again he was disappointed, and left the room sulkily, without anything more to say.

Arnold certainly could not complain of neglect. To the contrary, he was exhausted by more questionnaires, advisory consultations and therapy than he considered necessary. His daily treatment included supervised calisthenics and sessions under a sun-lamp and the vigorous fingers of a staff masseuse, therapies which were said to stimulate circulation of the blood and thus promote the healing process. Of course, every extra attention was an extra item on his account, which, while nobody yet mentioned the fact, soon exceeded the provisions of his insurance.

Although he was on the hospital's A-list creditwise, he was obliged, like the other inmates, to conform with the institution's inflexible time-table, which began at dawn with notification that the day had begun. Hospital régimes are devised for the convenience of hospitals.

After only two more days, in spite of the traffic through his room of all the specialists and their aides and student observers,

Arnold began to feel somewhat better. He ached less, though it was still an effort to hobble to the bathroom. He was able to see straight, and his speech sounded normal.

Then one afternoon, when he was anxiously facing up to the fact that he really should make some telephone calls to let people know where he was, there was a pleasant surprise.

29

"I'm so happy you're here," a nurse told Arnold. "Not happy why, of course, but happy I have a chance to get to know you." She was a woman who appeared to be in the full bloom of her early thirties, a brunette of charming dimensions and demeanor, one of those young nurses whose eyes shine with virtuous enthusiasm. There *are* such life-enhancing nurses, as well as the other kind, who seem to be taking revenge for some unforgivable grievance. The nurse who came into his room for the first time with breakfast the next morning made him glad to be awake.

"Well, if you're happy, I'm happy," Arnold said with a smile so broad that it made him wince. There had been nothing to smile about recently, and the wounds were still tender. "Any special reason?"

"Yeah, very special. I'm a besotted Squidgy fan. I started reading the Squidgy books to Rupert, my son, when he was five. I talked my friend in Registration into reading them to her daughter, so when she noticed your name she tipped me off. I nicknamed my boy Squidgy and it stuck. He likes it. He still likes the books so much at the age of eleven that when I had to send him away to school in St Louis after my divorce he took the whole set with him, for company, the way a child might keep a beloved old teddy bear. I mean, no kidding, Mr Bosworth, we are *serious*."

His ego these days was sorely in need of balm. He remembered how easily a flattering request for autographs had lured him into ambush. This time, though, the friendliness seemed entirely genuine, and he wanted more of it. They both felt a spark of sympathy.

"You know my name," he said. "What's yours?"

"Betty. Betty Plowright. Plowright's my maiden name. I picked his initial off my towels."

"Betty Plowright," he repeated thoughtfully. "A good, honest, straightforward sort of name."

"Thanks. I'm glad you like it."

She managed to switch her room assignments so that she could visit him several times a day. At first, she talked as a Squidgy fan—the same, in the thinnest of disguises, as an Arnold Bosworth fan. He looked forward to their conversations.

"I checked squirrels in the library," she said. "They're classified as rodents, the most abundant order of mammals. They're vegetarians. They breed litters of two or three, twice a year. American grey squirrels flourish close to humans, and are common in city parks. According to the encyclopedia, squirrels are 'arboreal scamperers.' I liked the sound of that and looked up the words in the dictionary. Squirrels run up and down trees and jump from branch to branch, mainly for the fun of it."

"There's a lot to be said for scampering."

"But squirrels are responsible, aren't they? They make sure their families have enough to eat. They're good providers. They get up at dawn and go collecting nuts and seeds and things. They bring them home in pouches in their cheeks and store food for the winter. A squirrel can live in the wild for ten years."

"You know more about squirrels than I do," Arnold commented with an admiring smile.

"The facts are interesting. But I prefer fantasy. My favorite story's the one about when Squidgy becomes invisible, so no one can catch him. And I like the one about what he has to do to survive when he shrinks to the size of an ant. He's very brave."

"He has to be."

"Do you identify with him?"

"I do a lot of wishful thinking."

She made him feel quite sentimental about Squidgy. Arnold missed him.

After a few more days the patient felt much better. His brain had recovered from the concussion. X-rays showed that no bones were broken. His arms and legs were normally mobile. A urologist pronounced Arnold's genitals OK.

"Ah!" Betty exclaimed one morning. "You've shaved. What an improvement!"

"But not yet ready for public appearances."

His nose was no longer swollen. The purple bruises on his face had faded. However, mauve and traces of sunset colors around the edges were still sufficiently melodramatic to provoke curiosity. Questions, no matter how well meant, would be embarrassing; and the answers, if truthful, would be ridiculous.

Late that morning, it was all he could do to nerve himself up to make a telephone call.

After not much interrogation, intermediaries put him through, from switchboard to switchboard, to Naomi Swartkop's innermost, private, personal office.

"Miss Swartkop is in a meeting, Mr Bosworth," the editorissimo's personal assistant said. "She's scheduled to be back after lunch. If you'll let me have your number? I'm sure she would wish to contact you."

All afternoon, the telephone on Arnold's bedside table remained silent.

"Isn't that encouraging?" Betty asked him when he confided that there hadn't been a call he expected from his most senior editor in New York, and that the lack of communication was causing palpitations and hissing in his ears. She smiled. Patients with high IQs exaggerated their symptoms. "If there's no call," she suggested, "surely there can't be anything to worry about."

"I do believe I'm going to order a bottle of wine with dinner."

"A nice thought," she acknowledged. "But—didn't you know?—the hospital is dry. The widow gave the money to build it on condition it'd serve nothing stronger than Sprite. Her late billionaire husband was such a difficult problem drinker he was expelled from Alcoholics Anonymous. Sorry, Arnold, no wine. Your disappointment makes me think you're well enough to move out of here. Think of the account you're running up! The extras!"

"How can I show myself in another school looking like this?"

"You don't have to stay here to complete your recuperation. You can move to my place."

30

Why? he asked himself. Was this the tender trap of song and story?

"You should get away from the institutional smell," Betty recommended. "Eat some real food. There's plenty of space in my apartment. Rupert won't be back from school till next month. You could use his room as a studio. There's a desk. Wouldn't it be wonderful if you could start the next Squidgy story?"

Why really though? Altruism is rare. What was he supposed to offer in return?

"I'm married," he admitted.

"It's all right, Arnold. I know. I checked with Registration. Next of kin: Cynthia Bosworth, wife." Betty laughed. "Don't be nervous. No strings. I'm not looking for another husband. I've been there. I prefer things the way they are. I'm only thinking of a visit. For the companionship, even a few laughs. And maybe you'd be willing to give me some advice on writing."

"Well," he said.

Why not?

"I mean thanks," he added.

Her apartment occupied the second floor of a redbrick mansion with white columns beside the front door, in a shaded garden, among yews and silver birches, on the edge of a tidy green park, close to the Nelson-Atkins Museum of Art.

"Nice place," Arnold said when she unlocked her door. "Very nice!" he added when they crossed the black and-white-tiled vestibule and she opened the door to the living room, which was decorated and furnished principally in the pastel blue-grey that was favored by French aristocrats before the unpleasantness of the guillotine. A banquette below a bay window and a wide sofa in front of a grey marble fireplace were upholstered with such exquisite discretion in antique tapestry colors that they would not have raised disapproving lorgnettes in the good old days in Versailles itself. Other features here and there, such as floor-length curtains of blue velvet, a mirror in an early eighteenth century gilded frame and an impression of Giverny water-lilies painted by the owner, caused Arnold to utter a gasp of grateful astonishment. The Monet alone was worth at least twenty times as much as the house in Annapolis.

"Anything wrong?" Betty inquired.

"No. Far from it. Your apartment is marvellous. No television. What a luxury."

"There's a room for that, and the bar. Shall we have a drink? Sit here, by the window. Relax. I'll bring them in."

He admired the view of flowers and a lawn smooth enough for croquet.

She returned a few minutes later, bearing a bottle of red Burgundy and two glasses on a small silver tray. He noticed the vintage, 1999, an excellent year.

"Is nursing a sort of hobby?" he asked between sips.

"Much more than that. I care about nursing. I suppose this apartment isn't quite what you expected of a nurse."

He did not meet the implication head-on.

"It suits you perfectly."

"My husband, the great Milion Koenig, was wealthy. He still is. He was the hospital's senior gynecologist. And he had a lucrative private practice. The best-heeled dowagers of Kansas and Missouri doted on him. He's a good-looking guy, and he can seem tenderly sympathetic when he wants. He's doing well in California."

"That must be an intimate relationship, between a woman and her gynecologist, closer to her relationship with her obstetrician."

"Milton kept a lot of his patients clear of obstetrics. He began operating when hysterectomies were ultra-chic. For almost every fashion-oriented, well-to-do woman over the age of forty, a hysterectomy was a must. And for every young nurse, marriage to a senior doctor was the pinnacle of success. Like flight attendants with pilots. In my first year at the hospital, I was only 20 and Milton was 39. He seemed all-knowing and all-powerful."

"Like God."

"No joke. In the hospital, he *was* God. His authority was irresistible, at first. I was awed. I became pregnant with Rupert right off the bat. A privilege, an honor, I thought. But disillusionment came all too soon."

Arnold nodded, marvelling at the ease with which female nurses and male patients can reveal themselves to each other.

"The trouble was," she said, "he was over-exposed to so many women from the waist down. After a long day at the hospital and in his clinic, he was sick of the sight of them—of us. Physically and mentally sick. By the time he came home, he said, his head was 'full of asterisks' only, of course, he didn't say asterisks. You can guess what word he used. Medical student's pick up a lot of crude language in school, and the words stay with them. Some doctors rationalize they have to act tough with each other as protection against the realities of their profession."

She sighed.

"I don't know why he married me, except as a target for his sadistic anti-feminist attacks. He said there was such a close correlation between a woman's 'facial lips,' as he called them, and her 'nether lips' that he could no longer look at a woman's face without revulsion. In the course of his examinations, of course, he often saw female genitalia when not looking their best. Unfortunately, he imaginarily transposed the symptoms of pathology to faces. He made me—a nurse!—afraid of disease, and ashamed of my body."

"Not very romantic for a young bride."

"A young nurse. A young nurse with ideals."

"Poor Betty."

"He was really vicious. He described all the disfiguring diseases a woman may be susceptible to. He enjoyed making me afraid. Eventually, I wouldn't let him touch me.

The abuse became physical. He hardly knew what hit him when he heard from my attorney."

She smiled and raised her glass.

"Here's to freedom!" she proposed. "You needn't look solemn. I regained my self-esteem. Things have worked out just fine. He failed to make me hate men. Here's to alimony! Here's to child support! I kept the apartment. Here's to Louis Quinze furniture! And, of course, he quit the hospital, and I kept my job. So I meet such interesting people. Like you, for instance."

31

On the playground of John Paul Jones Elementary, most of the girls and boys were engaged in childish pastimes, throwing and hitting balls of various sizes to and fro, activities no more meaningful than the games of grown-ups. Angelica and Bobo, however, were in conference. When others attempted to join them, would-be interlopers were told, in no uncertain terms, they were unwelcome.

"A one-night stand," Bobo was explaining with the authority of her senior status, "is when two strangers get together and screw for only the one night, then go their separate ways. An affair is different: it's when they screw over and over again, for maybe about a week or more. When did you last hear from your daddy? I imagine he's involved in an affair."

"You always imagine the worst," Angelica protested, her blue eyes shiny with indignant tears. "Not all fathers are like yours was. My daddy's not that kind of person. He told me he was going to be travelling a lot, doing research; he always does research before he writes a book. Cynthia calls his research goofing off. She would, wouldn't' she? She doesn't understand anything about writing. Researching is work, and when he's working work is all he cares about.

"Cynthia doesn't understand, on account of she's full of shit. I heard her phoning daddy's boss. 'Kansas City!' Cynthia said in that loud, rude way she talks. She thinks the whole world owes her. Daddy gives way to her on everything. 'What the hell's he meant to be doing in Kansas *City*? He must have turned his mobile off. Where exactly in Kansas City is he at *today*? Give me a number where I can reach him.' The answer wasn't what she wanted. She lost her temper. It doesn't take much to make her lose it. 'Not some time your secretary gets around to finding it,' she said. 'I want one right now, you dumb bitch.' That was when Miss Swartkop hung up on her."

"That Cynthia!" Bobo exclaimed. "She always gets up people's noses, doesn't she? But this time you can't hardly blame her for being pissed off. She probably suspects your daddy's hiding out for reasons of his own, and his publisher's covering up because he asked her to. If he isn't up to something secret, why is his mobile switched off?"

"I'm sure there's a good reason," Angelica said unsurely. "I suppose he's busy and he doesn't want Cynthia bothering him."

"Uh-huh?" Bobo said, with a provocatively sceptical grin. "Sounds like an affair to me."

32

Rupert's bed, temporarily Arnold's, was at one end of a long room. The studio was at the other end—a writing desk bearing a laptop computer beside an extensive bookcase, an easel close to a north-facing window; and, conveniently near that, clusters of paint brushes in pots, a wooden palette, obviously in service, and a row of tubes of oils, the full spectrum, on a work-stained deal table. A baby grand piano and an elaborate sound system completed the facilities for the expression of every reasonable creative artistic impulse. In one corner, two armchairs covered in red leather, a circular glass coffee table and a concealed kitchenette made it possible to take time out for refreshment and restful meditation. And, of course, Rupert had his own bathroom, with Jacuzzi. Arnold saw at a glance that he was going to be comfortable during his stay.

The first evening, he and Betty enjoyed a simple, light meal in the kitchen. Vichyssoise, a shrimp soufflé, raspberries and cream and an assortment of cheeses.

"A delicious soufflé," Arnold said. "Perfect!"

"Thank you."

"If you're on duty tomorrow morning, I suppose you would like an early night. But would you show me your work-in-progress first? If you prefer not to, I'd understand. Many artists won't show any one a painting before it's finished—sometimes not even then. If you don't want me to look, though, you'd better take it off the easel and hide it."

He managed a small, disarming laugh.

"There's nothing there I'd mind you seeing," Betty said. "In fact, I'd like to talk with you about it."

"I'm really curious."

"We can have our coffee in the studio."

There was no painting on the easel, only a large sheet of white paper, bearing written words, in big, loose swirls of India ink.

"This is what I do," she explained. "I compose in words, free and easy words, then visualize from there. I came up with this project at four in the morning, a couple of nights ago. My psychiatrist says this can be the freest, most productive time, when you're emerging from a dream state and your subconscious is still mostly uninhibited. Here are images from the depths of my id."

Arnold read aloud slowly.

"'Parade of Things, coming right at you. Dark, lumpy creatures. Small, red eyes. Floppy tentacles. That small, grey figure in the background, with a head like a hairy egg, is Senator Klumff's alter ego, a pioneer activator of bipolar forward planning symposia. They're a Foggy Bottom Focus Group, trying to figure out the most economical way of ending the world. Their agenda is already overflowing with squelchy old initiatives. The delegates are up to their ankles in yellow ooze. The naked bodies are grey-green and the sky is almost black with dense, intricate cross-hatching.'"

"Well," Arnold said. "That's some concept."

"Do you think maybe I have the gestation of a picture book for young children? I feel they should be warned."

"You're on to exactly the sort of idea my editor at Varoom! is looking for."

He said he would write an e-mail Betty could send to Naomi Swartkop to get the ball rolling.

"Let me sleep on it," he said. "We want to be sure you make the right approach."

"Oh, Arnold! You're a living doll. I knew you'd be able to help me."

She gave him a hearty Platonic hug.

"And I've had another brainwave that I'm sure would hit pre-adolescent kids where they live. I've been experimenting with Vomit Abstractions. Jackson Pollock pointed the way with his drip paintings. I'm carrying on a logical step forward."

"Yes?" Arnold said doubtfully, without actually stating doubt.

"I get big blow-ups of erotic photographs, printed in pale sepia, and place them on the floor. I swallow some bright vegetable dyes. I have two or three double margaritas—tequila's the best for a powerful reflex. Then I lean over the pictures and vomit abstract patterns on them. The effect is dramatic. When I figure out a way of fixing and deodorizing them, they'll serve as effective inoculations against pornography."

"Yes," Arnold said. "Very original. However, to start, let's just go with the Hieronymous Bosch approach and leave Jackson Pollock for a while."

33

Betty got the morning off with an imaginary suspected viral infection. After breakfast, Arnold and she spent nearly three hours in the studio, attempting to present her proposed works in a comprehensible e-mail.

"Naomi's one tough cookie," he warned Betty, preparing the way for what he anticipated might be an abrupt let-down.

"That's all right, Arnold," she assured him. "Your faith is sufficient encouragement. It means a lot to me. Don't worry."

When she reluctantly decided after lunch that she had better put in an appearance at the hospital, Arnold telephoned the Varoom! office. To his surprise, Naomi accepted his call without any delay.

"Hi, Naomi!" he began, as heartily as possible. "How goes it?"

"It goes all right. How are you?"

"I'm fine."

There was an awkward brief silence.

"Naomi. Earlier today, I sent you an e-mail, signed by Betty Plowright. Betty's a nurse I've got to know out here."

"It's on my desk. I've read it. Twice."

"Listen, Naomi. Let me explain."

She said nothing. He assumed she was allowing him to try.

"First, let me tell you why I haven't been in touch. I did phone a couple of times, but you were unavailable. I guess I should have written, but the situation was a bit difficult. I suffered a concussion. I was hospitalized."

"Oh?"

"Yeah, I was pretty badly beaten up. I visited a primary school in Kansas City and the children objected to some of the things I said. There was this vicious gang of fat girls—"

"I don't know why you think you have to make excuses, Arnold. So we haven't spoken for a few days. So? I haven't been holding my breath. Varoom! is a major operation. You aren't my only author."

"No, of course not."

"I didn't expect you to report on your survey every day. So some kids took exception to your opinions. They *attacked* you!

That's interesting, even if you're exaggerating somewhat. Anyway, I thought you called about the e-mail."

"I wanted to say something about that too. I'm sorry, Naomi. It must've made you think I've flipped. But Betty Plowright has been very kind. She was a nurse in the hospital, and then she invited me to recuperate in her apartment. She has a lovely home. Her ex-husband is a very successful gynecologist in California. Betty said she's enthusiastic about doing some picture books. I humored her, I admit. I felt I owed her something. Please forgive me for taking up your time. I realize her ideas come from outer space. I—"

"She makes sense, Arnold. She's a genuine innovator, and Varoom! is in the innovation business."

"But—"

"I'll write her soon, tell her. In the meantime, Arnold, try to think future. That's what you were sent into the field to do. And for Christ's sake call your family. They sound mad as hell and they keep cluttering up our switchboard."

34

"Fun and games in the Midwest?" Cynthia suggested with simulated excitement. In her natural (sour) voice, she added: "Guess what. I couldn't care less. You can do what or who you like. I was only slightly curious where you've been hanging out these last few days. I didn't know whether to send a detective or make a claim for insurance."

Her telephone manner was often sarcastically aggressive or sweetly cajoling. On this occasion aggressive. His was feebly indignant.

"I wouldn't describe my time here as 'fun and games,'" he said. "I had a bad time in hospital. At first, the doctors thought there might be brain damage."

"What would have been the difference?"

He began relating the story of the fourth-grade ambush, but she was no more impressed than his editor had been. Less, if that was possible. Cynthia uttered one of her most offensive staccato laughs, like the bark of a seal with laryngitis, disrupting the narrative flow. He had forgotten how hostile her laughter could sound at its worst.

"A bunch of little nine-year-olds put you in hospital," she said. "The naughty little things."

"They certainly weren't little."

"The naughty big things then. Corn-fed, no doubt. Come off it, Arnold. Tell me another one. Try the truth."

"OK. Here's the difficult bit. I don't suppose you'll believe this, but a nurse kindly invited me to recuperate in her apartment near the hospital. While her son's away at school, I've been able to use his room. It's a studio. She's very interested in the arts."

"Sure. A lot of sympathy. And, as the old saying goes, a stiff prick has no conscience."

"I was afraid that'd be your attitude. She happens to be an unusual painter and—"

"I bet she has all kinds of talents."

"She isn't a nymphomaniac. She—"

"But she does her best. How is it Kansas-style?"

"It's almost impossible to talk with you, Cynthia. But Betty—Betty Plowright—that's her name—Betty is a good woman. There are such people. She has helped others before me. There's a limit to what hospitals can do. She has a strong commitment to her vocation. And, admittedly, she is trying to help herself find fulfilment through helping others."

"A real orgy of helpfulness. I'm sure it's all culturally rewarding. So when are you going to haul your tired ass home?"

"In a day or two. I'm advising her on a pictorial literary project. Anyway, there's another man going to move into my—into her son's room by the end of the week. She wants to contribute to the rehabilitation of a young guy who lost a leg in the Gulf. The VA does a great job on prostheses. He's close to management of his artificial leg. He thinks he's lucky to be alive, but not very lucky. He needs psychotherapy. Betty got guidelines from the Veterans of Foreign Wars. The VFW's national headquarters is situated in Kansas City. A counselor there said amputees need love. She believes she can give her amputee a sense of self-worth. He's just a kid really and he doesn't have a family."

"Sexy. Kinky but sexy."

"You have a sick mind."

"Let's not get into that line of conversation. On this fine morning in early summertime."

"Well, how are things at home?"

"That's the spirit! I thought you'd never ask."

"How are things? Is Angie all right? Are you all right?"

"I'll let your itsy-bitsy Angie-baby speak for herself. As for *moi*, I'm fed up to here. Do you know what? There's been a development since you went on your vacation. Jeanette and Woody are building a place in Martha's Vineyard. Actually building one. They have a top-of-the-range architect. They're up in Edgartown now, picking out a prime site. To get the view they want, they may have to knock down some old house. They aren't like you about antiques. You can imagine the smug look on her face when she broke the news. And she was so sweet. She's sorry for me. She has this great provider who gives her everything her heart desires. And I have you."

"He's Woody now, is he?"

"Elwood is his name, as you may be able to remember, if you

try real hard. His close friends and associates call him Woody. The Ersdales and I are getting closer and closer, while you and I get further apart. It's sometimes depressing, comparing them and us, our different life-styles. But educational too. In Washington, they move in a different milieu to ours. He's making steady progress with Senator Brocklehurst. I have to tell you, Arnold, I've confided in Jeanette, during our lunches. There had to be someone I could spill it all out to. To put things plainly, she thinks I'm out of my mind, putting up with the way you do things—the way you don't do them. What was wrong with Woody's generous offer to commission you to give an assist to Jeanette with a children's book? Don't you recognize what they were willing to do for you—get you out of your rut? So when are we going to get our Vineyard estate? Ha, fucking ha."

"If you've finished your speech, let me remind you I'm not about to become that woman's ghostwriter."

"Jeanette says I should dump you. She has called my attention to the fact that Washington is full of attractive, unattached men who could buy and sell you before breakfast."

"Can I speak to my daddy?" Angelica asked.

"Jesus, it's the brat!" Cynthia exclaimed. "Snooping again. Arnold, we'll talk when you get back. In the meantime, I'm sure you and the infant genius have lots to say to each other."

Cynthia slammed down the living-room telephone, and Angelica, unperturbed by her stepmother's animosity, retained the extension in the kitchen.

"You shouldn't listen in on other people's conversation," Arnold crossly pointed out.

"You aren't just other people. You're Daddy. I want to know what's going on."

"You aren't helping by making Cynthia lose her temper."

"Is she going to dump you?"

"Of course not. I won't let her."

"I wish you would."

"Angie, you don't understand."

"Yes, I do. That Betty—are you and Betty doing it? Bobo thinks you are."

"Bobo talks nonsense."

"She's my best friend."

"Even best friends sometimes talk nonsense."

"But you love Betty, don't you?"

"What has given you that idea?"

"Do you love her?"

"Angie, you're beginning to annoy me."

"Do you love her?"

"Oh, for God's sake! OK! Yes! I love her, I love her, I love her! Satisfied?"

Angelica quietly put down the receiver.

Betty was delighted to receive an e-mail from Naomi Swartkop, inviting her to visit New York immediately with "sample visuals."

"This could be the beginning of something big," Naomi wrote. "We at Varoom! are deeply enthused. Of course, all your expenses will be reimbursed."

Arnold called Delta Airlines for a flight to Washington/Baltimore.

35

Of the Ten Commandments that God gave to Moses to regulate a virtuous life, "Thou shalt not kill" is the one most flagrantly disregarded on every level of society, from the President & Commander in Chief of the biggest democracy in the world down to the lowliest voters.

The Christian Church, in its ecumenical wisdom, endorses what it calls "a just war." In a cause that God is known to approve of, a nation may justly kill thousands, even millions, of another nation's citizenry. Killing only one person, however, is generally disapproved of, even when releasing a sufferer from incurable agony. Morality is a matter of scale. Indeed, disapproval of free-lance killing is so severe that the state may judicially kill the killer. Although murderousness is not in the ecclesiastical catalogue of deadly sins, pride, covetousness, lust, anger, gluttony, envy and sloth, in different combinations, usually motivate homicide and manslaughter in their various degrees of punishable culpability.

Such considerations were not on Angelica's mind as her daddy headed for home. She was impelled to kill with love aforethought.

36

Arnold had not expected a brass band and speeches to welcome him home, but he was disappointed by what he found. Cynthia had sounded extra-disenchanted on the telephone, but it was her usual practice to exaggerate her grievances on the telephone when he was away, in order to prepare him to offer concessions when he got back, for the sake of peace. But now she was not even there. The only person in attendance was Belle, the live-out housekeeper. She was in the living-room, cleaning the already-clean carpet. When she heard him enter the house, she kept the Hoover going for a few seconds to show how industrious she was. Then she switched off; and, without any preliminaries, took the conversational initiative.

"Mrs Bosworth said you'd probably have something to eat on the plane."

"No, Belle, I didn't. I thought she'd like to go out for lunch or have it here."

"She said to tell you she had a previous engagement—"

"With Mrs Ersdale."

"Yes, sir. With Mrs Ersdale, over to Washington."

"I see."

"She said she wasn't exactly sure when she'd be back."

"No, I suppose not."

Belle evidently took pity on him.

"Do you want me to fix you some lunch? There's plenty of things in the freezer. I could microwave you a nice steak."

"No, thanks, that's all right. I'm not really hungry. How's everything with you?"

"I'm fine, thank you."

"And Angie?"

He tried to make the inquiry seem casual, but he was aware that the telephone conversations had upset her.

"She's fine too, far as I know."

"What do you mean, as far as you know?"

"Miss Angelica doesn't talk to me much as she used to. She's been spending a good deal of time with her friend Bobo. In fact, Ms Simmons will be picking them up again this afternoon."

"Who's Ms Simmons?"

"Bobo's mother. Mrs Bosworth was going to send a taxi to the school, because she couldn't go, but Ms Simmons said not to bother. She likes Angelica a whole lot. While you were away on your business trip, Angelica's been going to Bobo's 'most every afternoon. The girls do their homework together and have fun. A couple of nights Angelica even stayed over. Mrs Bosworth said that was perfectly all right with her."

"She did, did she?"Arnold muttered. "We'll see about that."

"What, sir?"

"Nothing. Just talking to myself."

"Yes, Mr Bosworth. You must be fatigued after your long journey."

"If there are any phone calls for me, get their names and numbers. Say I'll call back."

Belle smiled comfortingly.

"That Bobo's a good friend, isn't she?"

Bobo and Angelica were in the Simmons kitchen, concocting experimental milk shakes with honey and blackcurrant jam, and talking about sex.

"It's men's nature, doing what they do," Bobo said. "If they didn't, how could there be any evolution? You can't really blame them."

"Yes, you can," Angelica said.

37

Angelica said she had to go home. Ms Simmons and Bobo drove her back.

The front door was not locked.

"OK, thanks!" Angelica shouted, waving goodbye. "See you guys tomorrow."

She entered the house as her father and stepmother were engaged in one of their noisier rows. It had progressed from discussion to dispute to incoherent abuse.

"The brat!" Cynthia disgustedly announced, pushing past Angelica, who had hesitated in the living-room doorway, and storming up the stairs.

Arnold turned and gave Angelica a weak smile.

"Sorry, Angie. I didn't hear you come in. It wasn't really as bad as it must have sounded."

Angelica did not say anything. She left the room and followed

Cynthia up the stairs. Cynthia slammed her bedroom door. Angelica closed hers quietly.

The house was silent, except for a serene Chopin étude, which, on this occasion, conveyed a sense of bitter irony. Arnold, subdued, looked at his watch. It was early, but he headed for his bamboo bar. He thought of Naomi, Betty and Cynthia, and groaned.

Angelica lay on her back on her bed, thinking hard. Daddy had broken his promises to her—faithful love for ever and all that. Her stepmother was a dangerous threat: in Angelica's imagination, banishment to a boarding school would be as bad as committal to an orphanage. Something had to be done. Angelica already had a plan. It was drastic but quite simple.

Oblivon is probably the most reliably effective soporific the pharmaceutical industry has yet developed for relief from insomnia. The drug has the authority of the old barbiturates, without the morning-after side effects. Without what Cynthia affectionately called "Barbies", she and Arnold would have suffered from fretful bouts of consciousness, on and off, all through the night. Episodes of mutual awareness in the small hours before dawn would have been even worse than the growing antagonism of the day. Neither of them made any attempt to break the habit of each taking two of the pink and green capsules every evening.

Early the next morning, before the grown-ups were awake, Angelica tip-toed nimbly down to the library. There on Daddy's desk was the white plastic vial containing the *Oblivon*. Angelica shook out four capsules and hurried back upstairs.

Even having had only the customary dose, Arnold was slightly late for breakfast.

"Sorry, Angie pet," he said. "We'll have to make our breakfast very quick."

"It's all right," she said. "I've had mine. It's time for me to go to school."

"OK. I'll have something later. Let's go."

"No need for you to bother. Ms Simmons and Bobo are picking me up. It's our new routine." Louise Simmons regarded Angelica as a sort of heiress, worth getting close to.

Sure enough, at that moment there were two blasts on a horn.

"No goodbye kiss?" he said. Angelica ignored the suggestion, and the front door closed behind her, leaving him standing in the hall, looking flat-footed and puzzled.

Belle arrived at 10 o'clock. There wasn't much clearing up to do in the kitchen.

"Mrs Bosworth hasn't come down yet," Arnold told the housekeeper, "but you can do my bedroom."

As she made the guestroom bed he had slept in, she disapprovingly shook her head and tut-tutted. She did not like to see this symptom of marital discord.

"My oh my!" she said, moving to bring order to the guest bathroom. "I do declare." The Bosworths were beginning to remind Belle of the domestic strife of her childhood on the Eastern Shore.

38

The Happy Hour was not as happy as Arnold had hoped. The Simmons did not drop Angelica at her front door till 6.20. She looked in at the living room. Arnold was in his favorite armchair by the fireplace-without-a-fire. Angelica observed he had already made his first vodka martini, with a neatly sliced zest of lemon peel, the way she always made it.

"You're late, Angie," he said with a smile that was meant to be ingratiating. "They taste better when you make them. What a gloomy face! Is anything wrong at school?"

"Everything at school is fine. And now I have homework to do."

"But, Angie—" he began. However, she silently left the room. She had seen what she needed to check on.

Upstairs, Cynthia was at her dressing table, constructing a glamorous mask. She was meeting the Ersdales for an early dinner at Lewnes, in Historic Eastport, noted for steaks and Maine lobsters ("3 pounds plus"). For Cynthia, the evening's menu was not the principal attraction. She was counting on Woody for legal advice.

"I'm looking for a mega-settlement," she had explained.

"Chester Pinkney will get you Arnold's balls on a silver platter," Jeanette promised. Pinkney was the lawyer her friends always used for their divorces. She encouraged Cynthia with a merry laugh.

"He can keep those," Cynthia replied with reciprocal merriment. "I only want my full share of everything else."

Hearing Angelica pass by, Cynthia called out: "Arnold! I'm using your car this evening. Mine's being serviced."

When there was no response, she opened her door. "Arnold!" she repeated, louder. "I said—oh, it's you. Where's your beloved daddy? Drinking vodka?"

Angelica ignored the questions, gained the sanctuary of her room and locked the door. She had a minor but important task to perform. She had to cut open the four *Oblivon* capsules with her nail scissors and squeeze out the soft contents for easy assimilation. The pale-grey paste had a not unpleasant faint odor of almonds.

Cynthia returned at 10.40 after a most satisfactory evening of practical guidance. Jeanette was so pleased that her friend was ready to conform that the dinner had become something of a celebration. Woody was as generous as ever with the Dom Perignon.

Arnold was in the library, listening to the reassuring precision of Bach. Angelica, having heard Cynthia's homecoming, surprised Arnold by assisting at the late-evening ritual. She had poured his brandy from decanter to balloon glass, adroitly adding the *Oblivon* paste when his attention was distracted by Cynthia as she noisily entered the library for a little tipsy gloating.

"Your days are numbered, buster," she told him.

"I see you've been dining well. Party-time with your pals?"

"They know how to live. Meanwhile, though, here's your Angelica, so how about my hot chocolate? I gotta have my beauty sleep. Or is that too much to ask?"

"Here you are," Angelica said, and passed her the steaming drink, fortified with its special double dosage. "We heard you coming."

Cynthia took the mug without thanks.

"I'll leave you to your boring music, Arnold, your boozing, and whatever you and your creepy daughter get up to when my back is turned."

Angelica allowed her father and stepmother a couple of hours to fall into deep sleep. The pretty nine-year-old looked even prettier when she changed into a freshly laundered pair of pink pajamas.

Then she went' down to the bamboo bar and collected the knife. It really was razor-sharp, as sharp as a surgeon's scalpel.

Cynthia was lying on her back in bed, gently snoring, with her mouth open.

Angelica stood beside the bed for a while, just looking, with the intense concentration of hatred.

She carefully placed the knife's sharp point against the left side of Cynthia's soft white throat, firmly pushed down and all the way across to the other side.

Blood gushed, bright red, onto the pillow and duvet, some onto the hand that gripped the knife, but none anywhere else on Angelica. She was calm, steady and strong. Cynthia, almost immediately, died with a hideous gurgle.

Arnold was profoundly unconscious, still slumped in his comfortable chair in the library, when Angelica, moved by jealous determination, inserted the bloody handle of the knife into his right hand. She pressed his fingers and thumb tight.

In her bathroom, she took off the rubber gloves, washed her hands and thoroughly rinsed the basin, and made sure there wasn't a single drop of blood on her pajamas and slippers.

Then, back downstairs, with a firm forefinger she rang 911.

39

At 1.17 a.m., police responded in two patrol cars with dramatic speed, ululating sirens, revolving lights and squealing tires. Each white car was embellished with a horizontal stripe of navy blue and gold—a characteristic touch of Annapolitan elegance.

The uniformed officers who leaped to Arnold Bosworth's desirable bijou residence were impressed by the dignity of the little girl who opened the door.

"Where's your daddy?" asked a sergeant. He had a young daughter of his own and was disturbed by the sight of Angelica in pajamas and a white terry robe, nervously blinking in the middle of the night.

"He's asleep."

"Asleep! How about your mom?"

"I explained about her on the phone, " Angelica patiently pointed out. "She's the person who's dead."

"Was it you phoned in the alarm?"

"Yes."

"This'd better not be a joke."

"No," she assured him. "It isn't a joke."

She led them up to inspect Cynthia, and down to inspect Arnold, and the officers were convinced.

A team of expert technicians was summoned from the Anne Arundel County Police Evidence Collection Unit. A police doctor pronounced Cynthia dead and Arnold unconscious. The couple were left unmoved until blood specimens were taken from Cynthia and her bedding and from Arnold. A woman technician wearing surgical gloves gathered the bloody knife, which had dropped to the floor beneath Arnold's hand, and wrapped what was considered possibly to have been the murder weapon (if, indeed, death had been caused homicidally) in a prophylactic transparent plastic bag for removal to the forensic laboratory. A police photographer shot pictures from all angles in both relevant rooms. Outside the front of the house, a cordon of yellow tape signified that the premises were now an official crime scene. The barrier was fixed in place in time to keep out a well-known crime reporter, who resented this denial of immediate media access.

"I'm from *The Capital*," he said, showing his press card to a nervous rookie guarding the door. "It's my duty to let the public know what has happened here. I've been monitoring your radio calls."

The reply did little to allow Freedom of Information and exercise of the rights guaranteed by the First Amendment:

"There'll be a briefing later at the station house."

"Perhaps," the reporter said in a voice intended to wither, "you don't know who I am."

"No I don't."

"I have a right—"

"Why don't you fuck off?" the officer inquired.

Everything was done with meticulous procedural observance,

as if the cause of Cynthia's death had not seemed obviously apparent at first glance.

The body eventually was wrapped in a black plastic sack and loaded on a stretcher and carried out to an ambulance. Efforts to awaken Arnold were unsuccessful.

"How much liquor do you think he's had?" one officer asked another. The other sniffed the remnant in the decanter.

"Smells like good stuff though."

So Arnold, too, had to be stretchered out. He was taken away separately, of course, in a van, because he was under arrest, on suspicion, even though it had been impossible to read him his rights.

Several hours later, in daylight, he came to his senses on a narrow steel bed in a bare white cell measuring approximately 10 feet by 10 by 10.

He rapped with his knuckles on the door and it was soon opened.

"What happened? Where am I?" he asked the turnkey, a paternalistic veteran of the force with short grey hair and a ruddy complexion, whose beefy corpulence was tightly confined by a hand-tooled Texan cowboy belt fastened with a massive silver buckle.

"You are in the Anne Arundel County Detention Center, located on Jennifer Road, in Annapolis. They say there are indications you knocked off your old lady. They say you really tied one on after doing the deed." The turnkey shook his head slowly, once to and fro, smiling in sympathetic wonderment. After all the cases of rape and child molestation, uxoricide (wife murder) was like a breath of fresh air. It is well known that even respectable citizens sometimes imagine killing their wives, whereas some wives imagine killing their husbands. The turnkey's fantasies had occasionally, not often, run along those lines. He was an experienced observer of human nature, including his own. He was philosophical about it, otherwise his job would have been intolerable.

"You must feel kind of rough," he said. "Wanna coffee?"

As a former student of Mencken's *American Language*, Arnold favored plain speech, particularly in situations as dire as the present one seemed to be.

"What d'you mean, knocked off my old lady? What sort of talk is that? Why am I here? Can't a man have a drink in his own home? Did my wife complain to the *police*, for God's sake?"

"If she did, she won't complain again. They say you used a knife on her so her complaining days are over. Why you're here, Arnold, is because you sliced her from ear to ear. You are here for a possible charge of first-degree homicide, Arnold. Murder one, as we say in the trade."

"You have a twisted sense of humor, er—"

"You can call me Clem. I'm not judgemental and I don't go for formality, even with guys accused of murder. There's always a psychological reason for murdering a spouse. There are provocations, am I right?"

"Listen, Clem. Give me a break. I admit I may have had too much to drink yesterday. I have a headache and an acid stomach. Don't you think that's punishment enough? So do me a favor—"

"You have to face the facts, Arnold," the turnkey said in a somewhat more severe tone of voice. "Investigating officers found your wife in bed with a terminal wound, like she was stabbed to death. They found you with the weapon. I'm sorry, Arnold." The voice was almost friendly again. "They say it's an open and shut case. You'd better get yourself an attorney who's good at thinking up mitigation, the type of excuses that could make a jury believe you had a tough childhood. You might get away with manslaughter. Ha ha. Personslaughter. In the meantime, there's coffee on offer.

I try to make my prisoners enjoy the benefit of the doubt. You aren't even guilty yet. Technically."

"This is ridiculous!" Arnold protested. "I'm not someone who goes around knifing women. I believe in non-violence in all circumstances. Where's a telephone I can use? I'll get all this straightened out. I believe whoever brought me here must have been kidding you. I assume I'm allowed to make a phone call."

"Sure you are, Arnold. You're allowed one call. Be my guest. Make it a good one."

Clem led him into the small office next to the cell.

40

Arnold called his house. He was answered at last by his own recorded voice:

"I'm sorry I'm unable to take your call right now, but if you leave a message after the tone I'll get back to you as soon as possible."

There was a *beep*.

"Thanks a lot, Arnold," Arnold said. "You're a big help." Kafka, he thought, could have done quite a number on the Ansa-Fone, about a man who wakes up one morning to find he has metamorphosed into a recording device, like a clerk in a government office. It was funny, Arnold reflected without even a faint glimmer of amusement, how people cite Kafka when life awake resembles a nightmare. Squidgy was lucky never to have to depend on recordings. Arnold wondered whether one was aware of change when one was going mad. He instructed himself to pull himself together.

"That doesn't count as a call, does it?" he asked Clem, who was vigilantly standing by.

"I guess not. Give it another whirl."

Arnold obviously needed a lawyer. Annapolis was the habitat of countless lawyers of all shapes and sizes, so many, in so many competing firms, that they had to specialize as narrowly as rival academics. He had met lawyers in casual social encounters, but had never been sufficiently interested to discover whether they were corporation lawyers, tax lawyers, divorce lawyers, libel lawyers, patent lawyers, insurance lawyers, real-estate lawyers, lawyers who negotiated grotesquely extravagant contracts for pop musicians or lawyers who helped the rich and senile to compose their last testaments. The time had come urgently to get in touch with a criminal lawyer—that is to say, not a mouthpiece for the Mob but a lawyer as humane, liberal and (usually) victorious as an American Rumpole.

Giving up the search in his mind for the paragon he wanted, Arnold suddenly remembered his literary agent, Jeffrey Fenhagen, who was a graduate of the University of Maryland School of Law, as well as a nifty golfer, playing off 12.

"Hey, Arnie! How's tricks?" the agent genially asked, and then, without waiting for an answer, added: "I hear you've been brawling with schoolgirls."

"This is an important call," Arnold said, glancing nervously at the turnkey.

"To me, Arnie, all your calls are important. But I have to say I was beginning to wonder about you. You seem to have been dealing with Varoom! direct, without prior consultation with yours truly. It was only when I spoke to Naomi on behalf of another client that I learned of your escapade in Missouri. Fortunately, I was able to persuade her—"

"Jeffrey, please! There's a serious problem."

"Where's your survey of the teeny-boppers' new interests taken you now? Vegas? L.A.? Naomi said she's giving you *carte blanche*, up to a point. She's gambling on you, so get a grip. Where are you calling from?"

"I'm in Annapolis, Jeffrey. In jail."

"Boy! When you come out of your shell you really come out! What's the latest?"

"I've been accused of killing my wife. I need your advice."

"All right. Let's not play games. What is the situation?"

"I'm sure I didn't kill her. She had her faults, but I wouldn't do anything like that, would I?"

"Is this on the level? It's good to hear from you. It's always been good, all these years. I like to earn my percentage. Now, what is going on?"

"I'm in jail, God damn it. A Detention Center, it's called. You're my agent, Jeffrey. And you're a lawyer. So how about getting down here? New York isn't a million miles away."

There was a pause. Fenhagen sounded solemn, by his standards, when he resumed.

"I value you as a client, Arnie—as a friend. The Squidgy books aren't what they used to be. Times change. But I have faith in you. I'd like to help. But I'm not the kind of attorney who handles criminal cases. In my opinion, the smart thing to do is ask for representation by a Public Defender. They're eager and the price is right. Know what I'm saying? The Attorney General would fix it or someone in his office. In the meantime, I'll speak to Naomi. Knowing her, I'd say she's nothing for you to worry about. I'd say she'll be thrilled to bits. She likes her authors to be colorful, and, to tell you the truth, until recently you've turned rather dull."

"Naomi Swartkop isn't uppermost in my mind at this stage. I'm really concerned about Angie. My little girl. My housekeeper doesn't answer our phone. Surely, in the circumstances, Angie can't be in school. Or can she? As of now, I'm only allowed this one call. Will you make some calls for me and find out what's going on? I'll give you some numbers."

"I understand how you must feel," Fenhagen said in his professionally most emollient manner. "But this is beyond the call of duty, Arnie. You know how busy I am. I have a lunch date with a senior editor at one o'clock—"

"Jeffrey, Jeffrey, Jeffrey!"

Fenhagen could sense the tears of desperation. He was not an entirely callous son of a bitch.

"OK, Arnie. I'll do what I can. Take it easy, you hear?"

41

Within a short time that seemed longer, Arnold had some idea of where he stood: in limbo. Following the Grand Jury indictment, denied bail, he was committed for trial for first-degree homicide in the Circuit Court for Anne Arundel County, situated in Annapolis, at a date to be announced; his defense would be conducted at the taxpayers' expense, as Fenhagen had recommended; Angelica was reputedly in good health, at present residing in the care of Ms Louise Simmons. Why hadn't Angie herself let him know?

There was talk that the Maryland Legislature was considering, or was about to consider, the possibility of rescinding the penalty of death by lethal injection, even though proponents of capital punishment argued that lethal injection was said to be less fearsome than hanging. A survey of inmates of Death Row indicated that a majority favored lethal injection. Twenty-seven per cent, given the choice, would opt for a firing squad, and only an eccentric small minority (four per cent) would plump for the dramatic heroics of being beheaded by ax. In the meantime, they were all dying in the natural way, pending their appeals.

Arnold's agent and adviser had kept his promise to do what he could, which turned out to be quite a lot. He was able to inform Arnold that Ms Simmons could save Angelica from institutional supervision by the State if he would award Ms Simmons guardianship, and let her and Bobo live with Angelica in the Bosworth house, which was larger and more comfortable than the Simmons apartment and where, of course, Angelica would feel securely at home. She told Fenhagen she did not wish to discuss the proposal with her father, but to her it sounded "neat," and she was willing to go along with it. Fenhagen was working out an equitable financial arrangement with Ms Simmons as part of a written agreement. There was a clause providing for the child's return to Arnold's custody in the event that he should have the good fortune to be found not guilty.

Arnold's period of waiting was rendered less close to unendurability when a prison doctor said he would try to do something to relieve Arnold's insomnia.

"I am unable to prescribe *Oblivon* as such," he said in response to Arnold's request. "Evidently you are allergic to it, or so forensic analysis implies. *Oblivon*, combined with alcohol, might have triggered violence. Maybe *Oblivon* itself proved to be harmful in your case. Furthermore, it is our policy to steer clear of brand names. However, I'll see whether we can make available a tranquilizer synthesized in our own lab which would be appropriate to your capacity to handle drugs."

"When?"

"As soon as approval is forthcoming. There is a committee. You *are* in detention," the doctor reminded Arnold with a prim smirk.

Perhaps the most significantly effective innovation in the preparation for Arnold's ordeal in court was Naomi Swartkop's decision to make it a celebrity trial.

"It'll enhance the public's interest in Arnold's work," she pointed out to young Ray Pulaski, Varoom! Children's Books Vice President in charge of Public Relations. "Stimulating curiosity about the author is sure to give Arnold's sales a much-needed goose. I want you to figure out a dynamic PR campaign ASAP."

A couple of weeks later, Naomi summoned Ray to her office at lunchtime for a working sandwich and coffee.

"I'm not complaining your efforts to date have been totally lack-luster," she told him. "That was a nice piece you planted in *The New York Times Magazine*. But I'm thinking more ambitious. I'm thinking *Vanity Fair*, *Variety*, even *People*."

"Easier said than done, Naomi," Ray mumbled, squirming in his seersucker.

Typically, it was Naomi who came up with the big idea. Her intuitive understanding of the public spirit of the age was what had gained her recognition on publishing row (a Platonic concept) as a great editor.

"We'll have to get the trial televised," she said. "Remember how O.J. Simpson's Dream Team utilized TV and how much it did to condition public opinion and the jurors' perception of the rights and wrongs of the legal arguments?"

"I'm afraid all that brouhaha was before my time," Ray said with the irritating complacency of youth. The word that subsequently flashed around the office was that his admitted ignorance of important PR history was what thereafter designated him at Varoom! an ex-VP.

His immediate successor, clean-cut Julian Grout, was quick on the uptake and wore an orange and black Princeton blazer, which appealed to Naomi's sense of what's what.

"The clincher in the pitch for TV," he said, "could be the saying 'Justice should not only be done, but should manifestly and undoubtedly be seen to be done.' Gordon Hewart, England's Lord Chief Justice, 1922 to 1940."

"Exactly." Naomi was impressed.

"What would you say's the best way of putting that notion across in Annapolis?" he wondered. She liked this candid declaration of dependence on her know-how.

"They'll get the message," she assured him. "There's more down there than crab cakes."

"If you'll permit a personal observation, Ms Swartkop," he blurted out, as if admiration overcame the inhibition of a newcomer, "you have a wonderful way of putting a wise and complex thought in a nutshell."

Thereupon, she said he could call her Naomi. She treated him with some more of her bons mots.

"Tentacles is not a pretty word," she conceded, "but it aptly describes a major publishing house's sinuous lines of influence, with connections as tight as the suckers of an octopus. I tell it like it is. I'm not one of those pain-in-the-ass so-called literary types, who have no future. I'm a pragmatist, a realist. There are two kinds of novels: 'literary novels' and novels you see piled high near the entrances to leading bookstores, the kind people buy in airports to read on the beach. The same difference applies to books for children."

He nodded reverently as she warmed to her oration.

"To make a go of it in your new position, Julian, and I have a gut feeling you can, you have to comprehend our power and use it to our maximum advantage. And what is the source of that power? I'll tell you. It's simple. In this Twenty-First Century, everyone, but everyone, most notably every politician, every general, every CEO, every star of showbiz and sport, all of them, want to publish a book—not so much to *write* one (after all, what are ghosts for?) as to be *seen* to have written one or at least to have told it or inspired it. There can be few judges and legislators, if any, who would not like to see themselves in print between hard covers, especially during an election campaign, and in this day and age every year is a campaign year. You understand?"

"Oh, yes, Naomi! Absolutely."

Julian was not only intelligent, she thought, her eyes half shut in speculative contemplation. He was a good-looker as well. If he played his cards right under her tutelage, there was every reason to believe he would go far.

First he went to the Rockefeller Center headquarters of UBS-TV (the Universal Broadcasting Service), which was hot on the heels of the big three networks and gaining fast. His meeting there was not much of a test of his salesmanship, because Milt Siegel, the head of programming, was one hell of a savvy operator, who had already been shown a digest of the *Times* article and recognized the potential ratings value of Arnold's trial. The broadcaster could appreciate a paradox when it was called to his attention: the children's beloved fabulist was a wife-killer.

"We're cosying up with the Maryland Attorney General and don't anticipate any problem," Siegel said. "The Annapolis courthouse is an ideal venue—historic and state-of-the-art and photogenic as all get-out."

"I'm going down there to tie up any loose ends," Julian said.

"We'll be sending Honey Laverne from our Washington affiliate. She's carrying on from where Barbara Walters left off. Honey is ace on facts, and there's nobody in the business who can get more out of emotions."

"I plan to have a talk with Arnie Bosworth himself, on a one-on-one basis," Julian confided. "He's one of our longest established authors. He'll do anything we at Varoom! want."

"Co-operation's the name of the game," Siegel affirmed. "If you get to Bosworth in person before we do, you can tell him we've out-bidden CBS, NBC and ABC, and he'll find us very generous.

We ask in return he shouldn't present a too clean-cut image for close-ups. A little haggard will win him more sympathy from the viewers and the jury. Hair untidy, a couple days' stubble—you know. Tell him also he should modulate his voice when he's on the stand. Slow and low sounds thoughtful and sincere. If a speech coach can be got to him it'd be money well spent."

"Yes, I've already thought of all that," Julian lied. Siegel smiled as they shook hands in farewell. He admired an up-and-coming good liar.

Julian reported back to Naomi.

"UBS-TV is eating out of my hand," he said. "Their top man agreed with all my suggestions. He's super-perceptive."

Naomi's smile resembled Siegel's inasmuch as they were motivated by the same understanding of Julian's positive qualities.

"Assent," she said, quoting one of her favorite metaphors, one of her own creation, "assent makes the beautiful *swish* of a perfectly aimed basketball falling through the net without touching the hoop."

Julian was ready for Annapolis.

42

Thanks to Julian Grout's conscientious exertions on his mobile, Honey Laverne consented to visit Angelica one day after school. Honey almost always did a thorough, three-dimensional background check into individuals about to be involved in a long-running story. Arnold's trial, she had been informed, promised to be a top-of-the-range reality soap. UBS-TV was planning network coverage of each day's proceedings in court, plus human-interest interviews whenever the melodrama of the situation warranted. Honey was confident she was heading again into award-winning territory.

Like most of the other star TV interviewers, she had the chameleonic ability to change color, so to speak, to match the mood of any occasion. Bright and chatty in the taxi from Washington (the driver, a fan, had asked for her autograph "for the wife"), Honey became as hushed and unctuous as a funeral director by the time she addressed Louise Simmons at Angelica's front door.

"Sorry I'm a little late," Honey said. "Something came up at the studio."

"I can imagine," Louise said, who customarily put in about four hours a day, approximately the national average, watching television. "Breaking news was it?"

"Something like that," Honey said with a sigh of martyrdom and a smile of gratitude for sympathy. Actually, she had been delayed by a gin and tonic with her producer. "But this is no time for shop talk. How is little Angelica holding up? The poor little dear. She's a virtual orphan now, isn't she? I hope my coming to meet her here today won't disturb her."

"She's a brave girl," Louise said.

She led the way into the living room, where Angelica was sitting with the perfect posture of a straight back in a Windsor chair. Since getting home, she had had a shower, put on a pretty pink cotton dress, white bobby socks and pink sandals, and brushed her long, pale-yellow hair until it gleamed. She had decided against a pink Alice band, thinking it might be too much, even for what Louise had called "an important interview" and Bobo had hailed as "the big time."

"Angelica's as adorable as a girl can be!" Honey marvelled, quite sincerely. It took a lot to transcend her usual cynicism. She made this remark to Louise, as if Angelica were not in the room.

"Yes," Louise agreed. She was rather embarrassed, because she knew that when strangers praised Angelica's appearance, as most of them did, Angelica sometimes pretended to vomit behind their backs, other times crossed her eyes and stuck out her pretty tongue. However, this time was not ordinary. She demurely cast her eyes down at her clasped hands on her lap.

"Angie—" Honey began.

"Angelica," Angelica interrupted in a small but firm voice. "Only my daddy and my very best friend have ever called me Angie."

"Angelica then. I was going to say …"—and Honey went on to say what many people had already said and would continue to say about Angelica's delightful resemblance to Tenniel's drawings of the original Alice.

"Thank you," Angelica said, as if she were grateful.

"Well," Louise said, "Miss Laverne. Do you like Earl Grey?"

"Who?" Honey demanded, annoyed by the irrelevancy.

"Earl Grey tea. It's teatime. I thought I'd leave you and Angelica to get to know each other, while I made some tea."

"Thanks but no thanks. I'm not a tea person. I'll leave tea to the people up in Boston. But I would appreciate some quality time alone with Angelica."

Louise retreated backwards out of the room. Honey produced a small tape-recorder from her enormous, creamy Louis Vuitton handbag and patted a place beside her on the sofa.

"Don't be shy," she said. "Let's get together."

Angelica moved to the sofa.

Honey employed her usual technique, starting with a series of innocuous questions about Angelica's background, to relax her, then moving to the nitty-gritty of the foreground.

"Your friends must have envied you, being the daughter of the creator of Squidgy the Squirrel," Honey said.

"Except when Daddy loved the squirrel more than me."

Honey laughed.

Angelica scowled.

"Surely not," Honey said. "After all, Squidgy is only imaginary and you are very real."

"I can't explain," Angelica said, for she did not wish to expose intimacies that mattered. And anyway, how could this TV woman understand how Angelica felt about competing with any rival?

"OK, we'll move on," Honey said. "How did your daddy and your stepmother Cynthia get on with each other? Did they have many arguments?"

"All Cynthia cared about was Cynthia. If she didn't get her way, she lost her temper. I often heard her shouting."

"Did she sound angry the night of the tragedy?"

"Tragedy?"

"The night she was, er, killed."

"What are you?" Angelica asked. "Some kind of detective? The cops already asked me all that stuff."

"I'm sorry, Angelica. It's just that you are such a lovely, interesting girl I want to know all about you."

"I don't want to tell you all about me. Some things are private. I'm private. Aren't you?"

Honey was unaccustomed to disrespect from persons she honored with exclusive interviews. She clenched her jaws, unclenched them, and switched off the saccharine.

"I read a clip from the *Capital* which reported you were absent from your stepmother's funeral. How come you didn't attend?"

"I stayed in my room."

"You were grieving too much to go?"

"I stayed in my room because I wanted to stay in my room."

Honey irritably turned a page of her small notebook and tried again.

"I noticed Elwood and Jeanette Ersdale in a photo taken at

the cemetery, identified as friends. They happen to be friends of mine as well. I gave Jeanette a call. She said she was shocked by Cynthia's death, but not surprised. She said Cynthia and your daddy were about to split but your daddy didn't want a divorce. He was afraid he'd lose his house. What do you know about that? You're old enough to have noticed something was wrong."

"No comment," Angelica said. "Isn't that what people say?"

"It would be best for you if you told me all you know. I can help distance you from your trouble."

"What trouble?"

"*The* trouble. Your daddy's trouble."

For a fleeting instant, Honey's intentions seemed benign. But Angelica was not oppressed by awareness of trouble. Cynthia did not exist, and her passing had made the world a better place.

"I may even decide to interview you live, if I can count on you to level with me. There are some media people who accentuate the negative. You understand what I'm saying?"

"I think so. But I want time to think things over."

"All right," Honey said, "but there isn't all that much time." She switched that old charm back on. "Only promise me one thing, Angelica dear. If any of the others proposition you, remember I was first. I'll be your friend. Remember, I'm the one who can reach sixty-seven per cent of the American people of every race, color and creed, including Hispanics, from coast to coast."

"How could I forget you?" Angelica asked, though she was willing to try.

"It's time for me to go now. I'll keep in touch."

Angelica said goodbye and went to the kitchen for a Coke.

Honey exchanged a few pleasantries with Louise at the front door.

"That's some child," Honey said with one of her sincere smiles.

"Yes, she certainly is."

"She's photogenic, she has nice vocal timbre, and she's sharp as a tack."

"She has a high IQ."

"I'm sure she has. What is her IQ?"

"I don't know the exact score, but her teacher told me it's terrific."

"Angelica doesn't have much to smile about at present, but I noticed she has beautiful little teeth. Which whitening agent does she use?"

"She just brushes her teeth," Louise said.

"She uses the same toothpaste as me," added Bobo, who had somehow inserted herself into the departure scene and displayed whiteness with a big smile.

Honey ignored her and went out to the taxi she had kept waiting. Angelica returned to the living room with her Coke.

"That went well," Louise said. "Honey Laverne had nothing but praise for you, Angelica. She says seeing the case through your eyes could give her a whole new perspective."

"Jeepers! What a creep! Who does she think she is?"

At that moment, Bobo entered the room.

"She looked as good as on TV," Bobo said. "It'll be great, having her on your side."

"What d'you mean, on my side? I don't have a side. I'm just me. I don't need any Honey Laverne. She's a creep."

"You're right," Bobo said. "That's true. She is." However, Louise's manner was chiding.

"At Grammy time Honey Laverne's name is always way up there. Honey is one of this country's great interviewers. Maybe the greatest."

"Big deal!" Angelica said with a tilted grin. "What's so difficult about interviewing people? Anyone could do it. All you have to do is ask them a bunch of nosy questions."

43

Julian Grout was sitting at ease out on the private terrace of his room at the Governor Calvert House (1727), one of Annapolis's most historic hostelries. The sun was setting in the west, as usual. On a small circular glass table by his side there was a tall mint julep. Julian did not really feel like a Confederate colonel, but he felt pretty damn good.

He had been able to access Arnold that afternoon, and now he was calling Naomi on his mobile to report on what a fine job he was doing. Her personal secretary was able to get Naomi to accept the call without a long delay. Julian realized what the fairly prompt acceptance signified in terms of his status.

"Hi, Naomi!" he greeted her.

"Julian," she acknowledged.

"I'm not a *schadenfreude* type guy," he said, "so I didn't *enjoy* Arnold was up shit creek, but I couldn't help feeling a little bit gratified it was him in the slammer, not me." *Schadenfreude* was one of the three German words Julian frequently used to imply he knew the language. The other two (of course) were *Zeitgeist* and *realpolitik*. He also used "Brechtian" for cultural allusiveness. Together with his limited but choice French vocabulary, those few words, he liked to think, gave an impression of cosmopolitanism. They even suggested to himself that the four years spent in his New Jersey alma mater had not been totally wasted.

"So how was Arnold in himself, would you say? Is he up to making a good showing in front of the cameras?"

Julian hesitated. He didn't want to disappoint Naomi but he didn't want to offer false hope, which might mean an unfavorable come-back later. He took a guess.

"It's hard to say. I got the idea he is loth to reveal his emotions."

"He's always been kind of tight-assed. It's up to you to encourage him. He has to sell himself to Mr and Mrs America and their twelve representatives in the courtroom."

"As far as appearances go, however," Julian said, "he looks OK. He was wearing those coveralls? You know, those one-piece boilersuits. Red or orange, done up to the neck. Macho. The prison barber hasn't done him a favor. Arnold doesn't look like the portrait of the artistic writer on the jackets of his books. He's leaner. He looks younger. A net gain, I'd say. He doesn't have any complaints about the way he's being treated. Guys who kill their wives don't suffer from the opprobrium handed out to pedophiles."

"Did you tell him he's got to take every opportunity to plug the Squidgy books?"

"Certainly. At first, he even laughed out loud. 'This isn't some kind of publicity junket,' he said. I reasoned with him that his attorney could make Arnold's sentimental feelings about squirrels part of the defense strategy, an essential feature of his personality profile. 'Mention the books as often as you can,' I advised him. 'Some of the jurors will be parents, grandparents.'"

"Did he go for that? "

"I think he appreciated my visit. There wasn't time for him to say any more. Our time was up. His handshake felt sincere."

"I'll get Publicity to send down a batch of his books," Naomi promised. "He can hand out signed copies to the guards and so on. It would be beneficial to get one to the judge. Make sure Honey Laverne and her associates received the copies that were dispatched to UBS-TV."

When things went this smoothly, it was a privilege and a pleasure to work for Varoom! Children's Books, for Naomi Swartkop, Julian thought. He was proud to be on the team.

44

King Charles I of England granted the Maryland charter to the second Lord Baltimore, Cecilius Calvert, in 1632, and the State has been a fine place to live, even without slaves, ever since, a fine place to be tried, Arnold thought, under a juridical system based on English common law, a fine place to die. Ever since his earliest awareness of his identity and home, he had always been proud to be an Annapolitan, and still, in spite of his present predicament, he felt a part of local history.

Undertaking a history project at school when he was Angelica's age, he had studied the Maryland Great Seal and reproduced it, full-size, in India ink and watercolors, as exactly as his limited ability allowed. It had been an interesting but difficult task, which took most of a semester and earned him a disappointing B-plus. The reverse of the Great Seal was complicated, glorifying Lord Baltimore more than his grant. As a small boy, Arnold was awed by the seal and wished he had chosen to copy something simpler.

The escutcheon bore the Calvert and Crossland arms, quartered, surmounted by an earl's coronet, surmounted by a helmet with a visor as grim as a portcullis, surmounted in turn by an ecclesiastical cross and twin pennants—an edifice proclaiming aristocracy and its worldly and supernatural power. The shield was flanked by personifications of the principal sources of his lordship's wealth, a farmer holding a spade and a fisherman holding a fish. In addition to the Baltimore estate in Maryland, there was extensive property in Newfoundland. Now the Lord Baltimore is a hotel and Calvert is the name of a whiskey, but the Maryland flag displays the ancient arms to uphold seventeenth-century grandeur, and miniature facsimiles of the flag are available in inexpensive souvenir cufflinks.

A leaflet circulated by the State Archives showed Arnold that no tradition was beyond improvement. The Calvert motto inscribed on the scroll beneath the escutcheon, *Fatti maschii parole femine*, was translated for centuries as "Manly deeds, womanly words." However, the translation was recently deplored as politically incorrect and purged of gender offensiveness. It now reads: "Strong deeds, gentle words."

Paul Abercrombie, the Assistant Public Defender, a fair-haired young fellow with a monkish pate, usually wearing a Joseph A. Bank washable, charcoal-grey summer suit, fixed a conference with the defendant only two days before the trial was scheduled to begin. He urged Arnold to take note of how the old motto had been brought up to date in harmony with current ethical standards.

"Whatever you may feel tempted to say under the provocation of cross-examination," Abercrombie emphasized, "never, never criticize your wife as such. We don't want to antagonize the ladies of the jury."

"What should I criticize her as?" Arnold wondered, who was already beginning to experience a sense of impending doom. "A blot on the landscape? A fly in the ointment?"

"And please, avoid facetiousness at all costs. Image is vitally important. By the way, I recommend you pay more attention to your personal grooming. Neatly combed hair and a smooth shave will give the right subliminal impression. I'm afraid there's no way we can prove your innocence, but if we can put across the notion that you are essentially an innocent man, basically, there's a chance we can beat the threat of a capital sentence."

"Strange to say, the PR people at Varoom! suggested just the opposite. They said a haggard, unkempt look would arouse pity and sympathy in the jurors."

"I think I have a better understanding than some New York flack of how a Maryland jury responds."

"*Touché.*"

Abercrombie frowned.

"And don't try to sound clever. They abhor wise guys."

"Right. Haggard and clever are out."

"Let's get to the heart of the matter. Our best bet is to plead guilty as charged and pray for mercy. Dexter Bunn is not an unreasonable judge when he's in a good mood. I've detected a soft spot, but it isn't easy to get to. We must play to his paternal instincts. Mention your daughter. How's she doing? Has she come to see you?"

"She's at home, being well looked after."

Abercrombie did not persist in that line of questioning. He merely repeated himself.

"We must plead guilty," he said.

"What's all this 'we'?" Arnold wanted to know. "I'm the one who's pleading. I'm not about to plead guilty. I don't feel guilty. I don't think I am guilty."

"It's hard being in solitary. Loneliness can twist rational thought."

"I don't mind loneliness. Remember *The Birdman of Alcatraz*? I'm trying to establish a relationship with a cockroach. I've always liked *Archy and Mehitabel.* Don Marquis's cockroach is one of my favorite characters. He helps me keep a sense of proportion. He—"

"Yes, sure. You'd better rely on my objectivity. The evidence is very clear," Abercrombie patiently pointed out. "If there's a guilty plea from the start there's a chance, just a chance, I can persuade the prosecutor to moderate his demands. You're lucky we're up against Bernie Sachs. He and I were undergraduates together at Hopkins."

"How can that help?"

The attorney smiled at Arnold's naivety.

"There could be a *quid pro quo* if you cooperate. Are you sure you won't plead guilty?"

"Quite sure."

"As for character witnesses," Abercrombie said. "You haven't given me a lot to work with. I considered subpoenaing your Ms Swartkop, but fortunately I thought first I'd try a friendly, informal approach. After a certain amount of to-ing and fro-ing, I got through to her. She was reluctant—and that *voice*! She's too tough to do us any good. I decided we'd be better off without her. Can't you think of anyone that could be of some use? Image, Arnold, image. How about the minister of your church? You do have a church, don't you?"

"I sometimes take—I used to take—Angie to St Anne's. She likes the music. But I must admit I haven't been going regularly. I doubt very much that the minister is aware of my existence, let alone my character."

"It was only a thought," Abercrombie said, putting papers back into his black briefcase. "Perhaps the less said the better. I'll have to play it by ear. Between now and Wednesday though, have a good, calm think. Try to see the commonsense logic about your plea."

When Arnold was escorted back to solitude, he thought of the plea around the border of the State Seal:

"With favor wilt thou compass us as with a shield."

He did not feel optimistic that Paul Abercrombie and he would be thus compassed.

45

Annapolis's most exciting event of the year, not counting an outdoor musical production of *Peter Pan*, was weeks in the past. Another class of midshipmen had joyfully tossed their caps high in the air. Some of them, in the family-union euphoria of graduation, had already kept promises to home-town sweethearts and left the Academy as suddenly thoughtful husbands. Would marriage make duties at sea seem less onerous?

There had been a big boat show in the Spring and there would be a big boat show in the Fall. Summer was the season of slow news days. As barrels were being scraped, editors welcomed the prospect of the trial of a nationally known local author. A fatal domestic knifing was hardly the newsiest of items; husband-and-wife murders were routinely reported briefly on inside pages and in low-wattage FM broadcasts. But the fact that Arnold's home was only a step away from State Circle, the heart of Historic Annapolis, and was the author of a series of cute little books for children about a squirrel invested the story with unusual poignancy. Not only that; the preliminary research was as good as done: Arnold Bosworth was right there on Google; and Julian Grout's anonymous creative team, his writers, were posting colorful human-interest featurettes on the internet every day.

Publicity breeds publicity. The wire services picked up the story, embellished it, and disseminated it far and wide. Columnists commented on the disgraceful lack of Federal funding for marriage counselors. There were op-ed essays in *The Baltimore Sun* and *The Washington Post* on the long-term pernicious influence of children's literature on adult behavior. Stories such as the one about Little Red Riding Hood were overtly violent (not to mention the transvestism); there was covert incitement, no doubt, in the stories of Squidgy the Squirrel. The newspaper essayists lamented that permissiveness began so early that the evil inculcation was ineradicable—hence violence on the playgrounds, muggings in the streets, wars everywhere, etc., etc., etc. The thousand-word sermons were largely unread, but they provided a decent grey background to the lurid front pages and magazine supplements.

By the eve of the trial the media had tried Arnold and found him guilty. With the guidance of newscasts on radio and television, the public were well conditioned to appreciate the reality of the courtroom as entertainment. The executives at UBS-TV in New York congratulated each other on having tied up the TV rights to the legal proceedings for peanuts.

46

There was an avid crowd outside the Courthouse for the opening day of the trial. Since 1821, the Courthouse had grown with the city. The building's style developed from Federal to Georgian Revival and beyond; yet, even in its most recent enlargement, at the end of the twentieth century, it preserved a dignified continuity in the red brick of its splendid entrance archway, tower and cupola.

That sunny morning, with some of those small, white cumulus clouds that Maryland often does so well, the people who converged on the edge of Church Circle to witness what one paper called "Arnold Bosworth's fight for his life" were less dignified than the building. Many of them looked like tourists, in the sort of casual summer dresses, sports jackets, shorts and trainers they might have worn in Disney World. In their quest for amusement, there was much jostling in competition for space in the designated courtroom on the second floor. The majority were turned back. Sections of the public gallery were already occupied by the technicians and paraphernalia of television, three cameras, batteries of lights and serpentine entanglements of cables. Only a few early birds were able to get seats; the rest, like millions of others, would have to view the spectacle electronically. The rulers of ancient Rome pacified the mob with bread and circuses. Kentucky Fried Chicken and television are almost as satisfying.

In the courtroom, the TV light and sound checks were completed to a nicety. The Honorable Dr Dexter Bunn (Ph.D in jurisprudence) was in his private chamber, seated on his leather-upholstered swivel chair, which afforded him the intellectual illusion of seeing both sides of every issue—more, the front and back of it as well, for the chair could swivel through all 360 degrees. Now he was sitting there under the ministration of a UBS-TV cosmetician. The judge had accepted the TV company's offer of expert advice on personal presentation. He had read in a law journal how brightly illuminated complexion problems could undermine judicial authority.

Bunn had greyish-sandy, sparse hair, which he arranged sideways to cover as much scalp as possible; watery greyish blue eyes with pinkish rims; and greyish-pink facial skin, except where ruptured capillaries were beginning to redden his fleshy nose. But the cosmetician, whose beige linen trouser suit was butch-chic, knew how to encourage an anxious, middle-aged performer when he was about to go into his act.

"There's nothing wrong with your appearance I can't correct," she murmured with a conspiratorial wink.

"I've never had anything to do with any kind of make-up."

"I can see that. But don't worry."

She gently pinched a loose jowl.

"Basically, you need Max Factor pancake as a foundation. I have a selection here. I recommend the one which is most popular out on The Coast, in the motion-picture industry. Almost all the male stars of a certain age find it takes ten years off."

Having patted his face all over with a pastel orange powder puff, she examined him again.

"Much better," she said. "Next, I'm going to have to darken

those eyebrows a little. Their natural color lacks the strength your role demands."

"Not too dark. I'm a *liberal* conservative. I don't want to come across too right wing."

She smiled reassuringly.

"Your smile will take care of that," she said, causing him gratefully to smile in return.

The science of orthodontics is so far advanced that an adult's natural teeth can be as regular and white as dentures. When false ones are introduced they look as real as real ones. Bunn brushed his teeth three times a day, in keeping with the advice of the Council of Scientific Affairs of the American Dental Association. Nobody could have guessed what teeth, true or false, the judge bared in his rare, chilly smiles in court.

He thanked the cosmetics artist and shook her hand. He donned his black robe, with its touch of purple and scarlet signifying his doctorate. No, he immediately doffed it and restored it to the coat-rack. On this occasion, he would project himself as a human being.

Dexter Bunn was very human and a just man, in the tradition the *Mayflower* had brought across the sea with the Puritan ethos. He was open to the truth, within reason. Like that figure of Justice standing proudly upright above the Old Bailey, which he had camcorded with his better half on their recent vacation trip to the Old Country, he balanced the scales of pro and con. Unlike Justice in London, he wore no bandage over his eyes. It did wear one, didn't it? Symbolism was sometimes so obscure. Anyway, Justice in Maryland in the twenty-first century was not blind. He was as clear-sighted as could be. Judges, like everyone else holding public office, had to think of their political future, but he tried not to be influenced obviously by such considerations. He was lucky, he thought, that the sensational case before him, which had attracted the attention of the nation's media, was so simple, so open and shut.

As he opened the door from his chambers into the courtroom, he was fearless.

47

The courtroom was as familiar as a recurrent dream. Arnold had seen one like it, all the dark wood, in countless movies, television dramas and newscasts and in his imagination when reading about other people's trials.

The floodlights and spotlights, suspended from the ceiling or mounted on stands, were artfully focused on the flags of the United States of America and the State of Maryland, flanking the judge's throne on its dais; the witness box beside it; the two rows of seats for the jury, and the tables for the prosecution and the defense. Arnold's place, next to the Assistant Public Defender's, was lighted, he felt, with special glaring white brilliance. Looking down at himself in psychedelic clarity, as one is said to be able to look down at oneself in a near-death experience, he saw he was small, isolated among strangers, and vulnerable to scrutiny by the whole world.

"Hear ye! Hear ye!" ordered an anonymous functionary with a good voice, standing close to the door from the judge's chamber. "All rise!" Those were the only words the official was required to utter to inaugurate the morning session, and he got the most out of them, making the archaic authority sound very here and now. He had taken a course in public speaking in high school and was a zealous stage manager with the Free State Players.

The Honorable Dr Dexter Bunn, in a black suit, white shirt and grey tie, made a stately entrance, slow, deliberate, grave. He panned the whole room through his old-fashioned silver-rimmed pince-nez spectacles, taking note particularly of the three camera lenses, nodded in approval of the orderliness of the scene, and sat down.

"Hey," the unseen director whispered into his mike, "I like the glasses. Get in tight. They establish character."

"Good morning," the judge said to all in attendance. "Please be seated." He had the mild, not unfriendly but noncommittal mien of a bank manager contemplating a would-be borrower. "At this time the Court is going to call for trial Case Number S-08-117, State of Maryland versus Arnold Bosworth."

An uneven contest, Arnold reflected.

The director caused Camera One to swing away from the judge to focus on Arnold, a reaction shot. His face could be seen from coast to coast in extreme close-up, pale and shiny with sweat in spite of the air conditioning, his forehead creased by embarrassment and dread. Thus, when first displayed nationwide, his was the face of a man whom most viewers were likely to consider as guilty as the media had already implied.

Back to the judge. Aware of the political value of celebrity, he was even more long-winded than usual, and anyway he always enjoyed his star role, explaining the legal facts of life in easy-to-understand plain language.

"First of all," he said, rubbing his nose, imitating the aw-shucks imitation-modesty of James Stewart, "I must facilitate the empanelment of the jury. There are questions I will put now to members of the prospective jury panel. These are not my questions; they are questions counsel have asked me to ask, to find out information about prospective jurors' backgrounds, to enable counsel to decide whether or not they want the candidates to sit as jurors in this case. If there is something in their past or some belief that may prevent them from rendering a fair verdict, counsel would like to know about it. We are not attempting to pry into private matters. If any question should embarrass a prospective juror I will take the answer confidentially at the bench. This question-and-answer procedure is called *voir dire*, a Gallicism long since adopted by our judiciary. It means 'to see to speak.'"

The judge smiled a thin-lipped little smile at a TV camera shining a red light. He was gratified by this chance to display his erudition.

"Jesus!" hissed the director into his mike. "What is this? Some kind of high-school civics lecture? Go to commercial."

Millions of viewers were denied the completion of this phase of the judge's introductory words of instruction and were told instead how to solve the problems of many small debts by consolidating them into one big debt.

The judge turned to the prospective jurors and asked them, one by one: "Do you approve of capital punishment?"

The majority did. Two dissenters were excused from further consideration for jury duty and were replaced. One of those who approved expressed herself with great emphasis.

"Sure I approve!" she responded. "The guilty should rot in hell."

"The damned don't rot," a candidate beside her pointed out. "They burn, in flames that last for ever."

"Hell is beyond time," a third argued. "An instant and eternity are one and the same."

"Aw, don't give us that!" protested an indignant fundamentalist. "Read your Bible!"

The judge gavelled for order.

"This is no occasion for metaphysical debate," he ruled with a severe frown. "I don't want religious contention in this courtroom. Answer the question 'yes' or 'no.'"

"I like the hammer," whispered the director, addressing his sound man. "It's dramatic and it asserts authority. But isn't it too loud?"

"Much too loud," the technician agreed. "It's way above my acoustic range. I'm trying to maintain a nice sound level. The gavel ought to go."

"His honor wouldn't stand still for that," said the director, who was accustomed to splitting differences. "Have one of your boys insulate that thing on the bench the judge keeps beating on. Fix it with a bit of padding during the lunch break. I'll leave you to figure that out."

The questioning continued.

The Assistant State's Attorney demanded women jurors who were "real stand-up guys," as he described them, women who believed strongly in womanhood and especially the concept that women's rights were equal—at least equal—to men's, including the right not to be physically abused within the matrimonial relationship.

The Assistant Public Defender, on the other hand, insisted just as vehemently that there should be as many men as women on the jury, and that all the men should have been married for no fewer than five years. In the event that the death of Cynthia Bosworth should be shown to be the result of domestic violence, Paul Abercrombie, though not himself a veteran of the marriage state, wanted male jurors who sympathetically understood about female provocation.

During the process of dismissal and acceptance, there was only one more unseemly disturbance. When the Defense, through the judge, asked a man whether a husband could ever be provoked sufficiently to lose his temper with his spouse, a spectator yelled, "Are you kidding?"

Once again, Judge Bunn was quick to wield his gavel for order and warned that if there were any further outbreak he would instruct the bailiff to evict the miscreant from the building forthwith.

Words such as *miscreant* and *forthwith* were in keeping with the traditional dignity of the court.

"Frankly," said Milt Siegel, head of programming, to a couple of his trusted subordinates up at UBS-TV, "up to now, I'm a little disappointed. On a scale of one to ten, I'd give the wow factor a three, maximum. I hope Annapolis soon pulls the finger out or viewers will start switching channels."

However, more questions were asked, and answered under the penalties of perjury, until the opposing counsellors were satisfied that justice could probably be done in accordance with the Constitution and that Arnold Bosworth would probably be given equitably balanced chances of being put to death or not.

"At this time," the judge said, "we will take an early, ninety-minute luncheon break. The weather is warm, so jurors may wish to stroll down to the City Dock, where there is usually a refreshing breeze at this time of the year. If you do that, I recommend a taxi back, up the hill. I request—I insist!—that you do not discuss the case among yourselves. Avoid reading anything or listening to anything that may be said about the case through any of the media. Do not permit even your loved ones to talk with you about the case's possible outcome. In short, you are obligated to decide the case on the basis of what you hear and see in the courtroom, not what some print journalist or television or radio newscaster or commentator may say about the case. I trust I have made myself clear. You may go now, and I hope you enjoy the recess. The court will reconvene at one o'clock."

During lunch, UBS-TV ran a lively documentary feature on "Classic Murders of the Twenty-First Century"—there were already plenty of interesting ones to choose from. It was hard to imagine any viewers' being bored.

Nine of the jurors elected to spend the break in the Jury Room, where snacks were provided. The other three took a taxi down to the Marriott Hotel, on the waterfront.

"I bet his honor isn't strolling to lunch," commented one of the jurors, male.

A juror, female, who knew the hotel, led the way beyond the lobby to the rear of the building.

"We can have crab salad alfresco," she said.

"That sounds fancy," the second male said warily. "I don't want a whole lot of fancy stuff."

"Alfresco means we can sit outside and look at the yachts," she assured him.

"Oh," said the first male. "I thought Al Fresco was a character in *The Godfather*."

"Let's be serious," said the second male. "This is serious, what we've been selected for. We should have a serious lunch."

They were shown to a table close to the railing at the edge of the terrace. Several million dollars, in the form of a cabin cruiser equipped for deep-sea fishing and partying, slowly glided by.

"They do a very good ice tea," promised she who knew the hotel.

"Great!" said the first male. "That's *serious*. Let's get started. Now, who thinks the defendant done it?"

48

"It is alleged," the Honorable Dr Dexter Bunn told the jury, "that the defendant in this case, Arnold Bosworth, murdered his wife, Cynthia Bosworth, on the night of May 25-26 of this year. Mrs Bosworth was allegedly stabbed to death at their place of residence, Squidgy House, on Cornhill Road, in Annapolis. The charge is first-degree homicide. Bear in mind at this juncture that this is only—"

One of the male jurors failed to stifle a belch.

"I trust that none of you over-indulged yourself at the luncheon table," the judge continued in the superior manner of one who had limited himself to a single rye old-fashioned before his own lunch, which contained only the customary soupçon of sherry in the terrapin. "Well then. As I wish to emphasize, this allegation is only that, an allegation. The defendant is presumed innocent, of course, unless proven otherwise, no matter what rumors and speculations may recently have come to your attention. As you are about to begin to take in the facts of the case as presented in this courtroom, each of your minds should be a *tabula rasa*." He smiled one of his famous thin smiles. "A *tabula rasa*," he repeated, savoring the phrase, which, he confidently believed, hardly anyone else in the room understood, except the few members of the legal fraternity and sorority there present. After a pause, he condescended. "A clean slate."

To Arnold, the metaphorical slate appeared to be far from clean, and the scribbles on it were illegibly smudged. How could he feel absolutely not guilty or guilty when he could not remember anything that happened at the end of the evening in question? Never before had his memory been so completely obliterated.

"Mr Abercrombie," the judge inquired, "does your client wish to have the charge read aloud or is he willing to waive the reading?"

"To cooperate with the court, in order to save time," the Defense Counsel obsequiously replied, "Mr Bosworth waives, Your Honor." The regular performers knew their parts and the importance of courtesy.

"The plea is not guilty," the judge confirmed. He raised his eyebrows, bowed his head to gaze balefully over his spectacles, and, with a crooked forefinger, summoned Defense to the bench.

"Is that right?" His Honor muttered.

Abercrombie winced. The plea was absurd, as he knew and the

judge knew. In spite of all the last-minute efforts, Arnold had remained adamant.

"Yes, Your Honor," Defense said.

"So be it," said the judge.

Abercrombie humbly returned to his table, sat down and glared with unconcealed impatience at his client. Arnold apologetically, resignedly shrugged.

The rigmarole went on.

"In a few moments," the judge announced, "each side, State and Defense, will have the opportunity to make what we call an opening statement."

As the judge droned on, the UBS director sighed and considered inserting a commercial for a radical new driver with a massive square head that was guaranteed to hit a golf ball straighter and farther than last year's model.

"… the purpose of an opening statement is to tell you what the case is about, to fill you in on how the contending counsel plan to put their case together, to advise you on what they would like you to look out for."

"To hell with this!" the director spluttered. For a couple of minutes that were paid for by the second, the American public was denied the images of judge and courtroom while it was shown this season's champion on a golf course in Georgia.

"… one witness at a time until the State has presented all its evidence. Defense will have opportunities to cross-examine…. During the trial, almost certainly, one or the other attorney, from time to time, will raise objections. When they object, they will stand and declare, 'I object.' I may sometimes call counsel to the bench to find out exactly what an objection is about. I will decide: sustained or overruled. As one of my honorable predecessors explained the functions of a judge, I am like the umpire behind home plate. I will call the balls and strikes. But you, ladies and gentlemen of the jury, will be responsible for calling the final result."

Blah, blah, blah, thought the director. Most of the viewers, however, thought TV coverage of the trial, in all its thoroughness, was as educational as *The Judge Judy Show.* Some teachers who were closely attuned to the spirit of the age showed the trial on television sets in their classrooms. Thus, Bobo was able to watch it at school. Ms Simmons, at Angelica's request, got the Bosworths' family physician to write a note to the principal. She duly excused Angelica from attending classes, on account of "allergy to pollen," although her real reason for staying away was obvious. Angelica knew that if she had gone to school there would have been merciless teasing. She watched the trial in the library at home in deepening gloom. She was glad that school would soon be out for the summer vacation and she would have Bobo's full-time support.

49

Bernie Sachs, the chubby, not altogether unhandsome, youngish Assistant State's Attorney, left his table and approached the jury with deliberate portentousness, moving in the style he had learned from his seniors and major motion pictures. Grasping the lapels of his dark-grey summer suit, he parted the jacket sufficiently to reveal the golden key of Phi Beta Kappa and the incipient paunch of professional success.

He walked slowly along the full length of the jurors' wooden enclosure and half-way back again, making contact on the way with as many eyes as possible. A sense of intimate trust, he knew, won votes.

"Ladies and gentlemen of the jury," he said, facing them four-square and speaking in a mellifluous voice that perfectly blended confidentiality and public disclosure, persuasiveness and the authority of thespian conviction. "You are here to consider a most heinous crime, a preconceived, cowardly and cruel murder. The State will show you how a man drugged the woman he had vowed to cherish and stabbed her to death as she lay helplessly unconscious in the marital bed. That man," he said indignantly, as he turned and pointed at Arnold, "is the defendant, Arnold Bosworth, the teller of tales supposed to benefit the minds of the children of America. The woman was his loyal wife, Cynthia. There can be no doubt of your verdict. The State will present incontestable forensic evidence—the knife, State's Exhibit A, with which the foul deed was perpetrated, bearing the killer's fingerprints, his alone; DNA analyses of the victim's blood, the blood on the knife, the blood on the defendant's right hand; all the same. It will be painful for you to contemplate such a horrendous travesty of the marriage union, which we in Maryland hold so dear. But contemplate it you must, for that is your duty as citizens upholding the law. Your verdict can only be guilty of an offense for which capital punishment is mandatory. Let us then, without delay, undertake our distasteful but necessary and important task."

The State extracted a cream-colored silk handkerchief from a pocket and mopped his forehead.

"In Annapolis," he began, "the evening of May the twenty-fifth was fine and calm...."

After describing the events in Squidgy House, he told how the murderer's activities awakened his nine-year-old daughter, Angelica, and how the brave little girl, though she must have been terrified by what she found, was able to alert the police. He told of the rapid response of Annapolis's finest, with the back-up of medical services and the evidence collection unit. Everything was done according to protocol, with speed and efficiency. The whole community could be proud.

When Bobo returned late that afternoon, she was triumphant.

"It'll serve him right," she said. "He's going to get what he deserves."

"He's still my father," Angie morosely pointed out.

She was suffering from the first niggling discomfort of qualms.

50

The evening of the first day of the trial, Paul Abercrombie, Counsel for the Defense, at home in his bachelor duplex in a townhouse-style condominium in Chesapeake Haven, a new ex-urban gated community only 4.2 miles from the Bay, luxuriated in a long shower, hot, lukewarm and cold, until he felt all fresh and tingly.

With his fair coloring, he did not really need a second shave, but he did not want to risk complaints of abrasiveness. He eventually rinsed away the jasmine suds and stroked his smooth cheeks with approving fingertips and smiled at his reflection. He sprayed himself lavishly with Gucci's new fragrance for men, paying close attention to those special places whose condition can enhance a relationship or totally bum it out. With designer talcum, he powdered between his toes.

After careful consideration, he selected a Thai silk shirt from the stacks of shirts in his walk-in closet. Gatsby himself never had so many shirts of such exotic fabrics, such subtle colors. Paul chose ivory, which nicely offset his cornflower-blue hip-huggers and white huaraches. White! Yes, white. The whiteness was a surprise, from China by way of Taxco and an adorable little boutique in a location he planned to keep secret, lest everyone he knew would be wearing white huaraches.

Having lightly pomaded his pale-yellow hair and arranged a casual forelock and combed his eyebrows and swilled some mint mouthwash, Paul pouted coquettishly at the mirror, picked up his wicker shopping basket and set off. Destination: the residential complex at Westgate Circle, in downtown Annapolis. Paul tried not to mind that the address was smarter than his own.

"Oh, Paul, it's you!" exclaimed Bernie Sachs mock scoldingly, holding the front door ajar. He was wearing his at-home ankle-length Prussian blue and burnt sienna kaftan and Japanese wooden slippers. These evenings, he was indulging in a fantasy of Zen Buddhism, which was relaxing after the juridical fantasy of his working hours, and he believed the loose garment was flattering to the figure. "I wasn't expecting you," he fibbed. "Why didn't you phone?"

"I didn't want to give you a chance to say no," Paul said, with a smile he knew brought about dimples, which Bernie found difficult to resist. Paul conciliatorily added, "I stopped by Duke of Gloucester Gourmet to pick up some yummies."

Bernie sighed as if humoring an unruly but charming small boy, opened the door wider, and stood aside.

"You're really very naughty," he chided with a twinkle.

Paul went through the minimalist pale-grey living room he knew so well, to the convenient kitchenette alcove, and placed his basket on the counter beside the cappuccino machine. "There now," he said. "Stuffed vine leaves, smoked trout, apricot Danish and a bottle of peach schnapps. Summer fare."

"There goes Weight Watchers," Bernie objected in his ironic way of expressing gratitude. "I was only going to have watercress soup. Zero calories. You know you shouldn't have come. Apart from ruining my diet. We don't want people to see we're keeping company during the trial."

"Everyone knows we … spend time together. So what? Are you ashamed of me?"

Though they had been Hopkins classmates, there were irreconcilable differences. Bernie had gone on to Harvard Law while Paul had stayed in Maryland. Bernie was a year older than Paul and was now professionally superior. Prosecution is more glamorous than defense. Bernie could afford to be kind.

"Of course I'm not ashamed. It's just that they might suspect collusion. That suspicion could fuck up our careers."

"What's to collude? Your cases are sure things, without my connivance. Your boss wouldn't touch one if it wasn't. If we were operating in collusion you'd make me look good now and then."

"I see what you mean," Bernie conceded. "So let's collude on a whiskey sour. Or you mix up something summery with that peach stuff."

Paul mixed something up, and they sipped it, sitting close to each other on giant chartreuse cushions on the floor.

"I think I can help you put on a show with some look-good action," Bernie said. "An e-mail came to my office—it should have been sent to yours. It's from some woman in Kansas City. Betty Plowright's her name. She's a nurse. Bosworth was one of her patients. She says she could make a valid contribution as a character witness. She wants to help Bosworth. She doesn't seem to understand that helping Bosworth isn't my function. I could only use her to show motive. She and Bosworth probably had some kind of thing going out there. Why don't you enlist her on your side? A caring statement. Good idea? It wouldn't do me any harm."

Paul was grateful.

He made an affectionate gesture.

When they had finished doing the things they did when Paul visited, they rested together on the sofa, breathing in harmony.

"Maybe you'd better be heading back to your place," Bernie said, with a cavernous yawn.

"Yeah, I guess I'd better. Give me that woman's e-mail address first thing in the morning, OK?"

Paul clambered off the sofa and put on his jeans, with his back to Bernie, for the sake of modesty.

"I like the blue," Bernie commented. "Good with your eyes."

"But you haven't said anything about the huaraches."

"Oh, *bling*! I noticed them right away, as soon as you arrived. I saw them advertised in *Annapolis: 33 Great Ways to be An Annapolitan*."

Paul looked horrified.

"You did?"

"Just kidding," Bernie assured him. "Paul, you're too much."

They both looked forward to an amicable confrontation in the courtroom.

51

The case against Arnold Bosworth was being presented in inexorable, incontrovertible fashion. To complement the dry legalities of the process, the TV cameramen, beyond proactive planning, as usual, were exerting creative initiative, spontaneously revealing those details of appearance and behavior which demonstrate that even the most august of institutions is composed of individual human beings. There were zoom close-ups, for instance, of a forefinger excavating a nostril, a low neckline exposing cleavage, a juror whispering into the ear of an associate. Shots of such intimacy offered the best portraits of advocates and their courtroom entourage since Daumier. The TV coverage was sufficiently colorful to maintain viewing figures just adequate to satisfy the advertisers, and to establish Arnold Bosworth as America's Number One Villain of the Week. But only just.

"Dramaturgically," said Milt Siegel, up in New York, "this story's a tough ask. Where's the tension? The suspense? That Assistant State's Attorney What's-His-Name already has the killer well and truly nailed. The public has already made up its mind. All the e-mails and text messages say 'Guilty.' We need controversy, an emotional debate, or I'm going to have to pull us out of there by the end of the week."

"But chief—"

"But nothing. I'm beginning to feel distinctly unhappy." Siegel's lieutenant shuddered. Siegel always shared his unhappiness with the staff. Worry about their job security kept them on their toes.

"By the way," Siegel demanded in a voice of threateningly false politeness, "may I ask how our plans are shaping up to cover the LA gay fuzz drag ball? It's this Saturday, isn't it?"

On the production side of television, there is never any relief from pressure. The planners' brains have to concentrate fragmentarily on several projects at once.

"In the meantime," he concluded, "get me Honey Laverne on the phone. I mean, like now."

Mr and Mrs Viewer, not to mention all the junior viewers, don't appreciate how much goes on behind the scenes to keep the quality of the product up to standard. To give but one example, there's a back-room technical team that does nothing but edit and mix recorded applause and laughter.

"Honey," Siegel said in his automatically contrived expression of disarming counterfeit friendship, when the network's star inquisitor had been traced, procured and patched through to his line. She was in a studio Mercedes en route from DC to Annapolis. "I'm looking forward to your exclusive death-row feature on Albert Bosworth."

"Arnold Bosworth isn't on death row yet."

"I said I'm looking forward. I hope you're looking forward with equal enthusiasm. You know, we have to anticipate. Anticipate, Honey!"

"Naturally, I have the Varoom! people doing all they can to persuade Arnold to give me access. But it isn't only a question of what *he* is prepared to go along with. There are rules."

"Rules? That doesn't sound like you, Honey. "

"I'll get on to the powers that be again today."

"Powers that be? Honey, that's us."

He awarded her an encouraging chuckle.

She responded with a low-volume chuckle of well-conditioned sycophancy.

"Yes, M.S. I'll remind them."

52

Paul Abercrombie had not informed Arnold that Betty Plowright would be called to the stand to testify in his behalf. What, he asked himself, could she possibly say in mitigation? Anyway, surely, there was no way she could influence the jury to pronounce him only slightly guilty.

Arnold had not noticed her sitting at the back of the rows of spectators. As she walked confidently down the aisle, across the center of the courtroom, to the seat between the judge and the jurors, he and everyone else in the room sat up more attentively.

Her figure mocked the confinement of her close-fitting, grey-and-white seersucker suit. It did not conceal her ripe womanliness, radiating health and beauty worthy of an Olympic gold medal, an Academy Award Oscar. Voluptuous, buxom, *zaftig* were some of the words that came to Arnold's mind. *Zaftig* was his favorite: it was Yiddish for well-rounded, curvaceous, from the German for juicy. Wasn't etymology wonderful? Statuesque was another of the *mots justes*—statuesque on a minor scale. She was a compact

Venus, with arms. The sight of her made Arnold forget for a moment the anxiety about his fate. In the hospital in Missouri, when he was bruised and helpless, he saw her as an angel of mercy, a mother nurse. In her apartment, she became his literary apprentice, dependent on his guidance, and grateful for it. In the courtroom, her glossy, dark-brown hair was tied back in a demure ponytail; her naturally black eyebrows looked sincerely earnest, and she wore no make-up. Even so, there was no disguising the fact that she really was quite a dish.

In response to Defense's questions, this most charming character witness gave the court her name, place of residence and occupation, and testified that the defendant impressed her as brave, decent, gentle and kind—not the sort of person, no matter what the provocation, who would ever commit an act of violence. She seemed willing to continue to enumerate Arnold's virtues, on and on, but Judge Bunn intervened. Enough, he ruled, was enough. Her assessment was sufficiently clear. The time at the court's disposal was not unlimited. Did the State wish to cross-examine?

The State certainly did so wish.

On the way back to his table, Abercrombie gave Bernie Sachs a little frown of appeal to go easy, but Bernie, in his professional persona, offered no assurance as he passed his off-duty companion. Bernie's face was enigmatic as he confronted the witness.

"I am sure," he said in a tone of sweet sarcasm, "that all of us here today are touched by Miss Plowright's loyal eulogy to her ... patient. But Arnold Bosworth was obviously much more to her than that. Miss Plowright, is it not true that you and Arnold Bosworth were lovers?"

At the TV set in Cornhill Street, Bobo nudged Angie in the ribs.

"I told you!" Bobo said.

In the courtroom, Betty compressed her lips, then decompressed them to say, with as much emphasis as the word can bear:

"No."

"Perhaps I should approach that delicate matter more circumspectly," Bernie Sachs allowed. "Please tell the court where Bosworth moved immediately after he left your hospital."

"He came to stay in my apartment. To recuperate. He had been severely beaten and he was still shaky."

"Was that a doctor's observation or only your opinion?"

"I believed that he was fit to be discharged from the hospital but would benefit from further rest."

"Is it your customary practice to take in men after the hospital has finished with them?"

Sachs got the laugh he expected. The judge hammered with his gavel.

"This is a trial on a charge of first-degree homicide," he said. "I will not tolerate unseemly disturbances."

Sachs nodded in solemn agreement.

"No, it is not my customary practice," Betty said.

"Then this was an unusual invitation to one of your erstwhile patients?"

"Yes, you could say that."

"I do say that. I would call your invitation most unusual. Tell me, Miss Plowright, how do you rate Arnold Bosworth's attractiveness as a man? Below average? Average? Or above average?"

"Objection!" protested Abercrombie. "Irrelevant." What was Bernie up to?

"What is the purpose of this line of questioning?" the judge asked Sachs.

"Its purpose will become apparent very soon, Your Honor. It is central to the case."

"Very well. Objection overruled."

"Thank you, Your Honor. Miss Plowright, kindly answer the question."

"It's a silly question. As anyone in this room with eyes in their head can see, Arnold Bosworth's attractiveness is away above average."

"It is your opinion I'm interested in, but I imagine most other ladies would endorse it. By general standards, the defendant certainly is a very attractive man."

"Mr Sachs...." the judge said warningly.

Abercrombie peevishly clenched his jaw.

"Please bear with me, Your Honor. I'm about to make a crucial point."

"Make it without delay. I am not presiding over a Mr World contest."

There was more laughter, but this time there was no reprimand. The judge did not object to audience appreciation when it was directed his way. He might have classified the disturbance as seemly. It wasn't as loud as the laughter that punctuates a sitcom.

"No, Your Honor," the State acknowledged. "And I'm not nominating Miss Plowright for the title Miss World. But she, too, by current criteria, is unquestionably of above-average attractiveness. I submit that when she and Arnold Bosworth were sharing her apartment it is unlikely they were only playing Scrabble. During the days the defendant stayed there, they were very probably cohabiting in the full legal sense of that term, and a relationship rapidly developed that made Bosworth wish he didn't have a wife. Clearly, there was a compelling motive to do away with her."

"Objection!" Abercrombie cried. "Speculation."

"Overruled."

"Remember you are under oath, Miss Plowright," Sachs pointed out. "You are obliged to tell the whole truth. Did you come here on account of some civic duty or because of a more personal emotional attachment? Let me put a simple question. Do you love Arnold Bosworth?"

She turned to the judge.

"Do I have to answer that?" she wanted to know.

"Yes. Answer the question."

"Yes then. I love him."

Arnold was aware of a heatening of his cheeks, a prickling at the nape of his neck, a quickening of his pulse—in short, a glow.

"There!" crowed Bobo. "She admits it."

"What's wrong with loving someone?" Angie said.

"And Arnold Bosworth loved you, didn't he?" the State insisted.

"I don't think so," Betty said. "He never suggested anything like that. He thanked me, that's all. In gratitude, he helped me prepare my work for submission to Varoom!, his publisher. What you call our relationship was simply friendship on a completely innocent, platonic level."

She smiled wistfully and added:

"Worse luck for me. He's a perfect gentleman."

Bernie Sachs scowled.

"No further questions," he said.

The State's next volunteer witness was more helpful to him.

There was a stirring of revived interest in the courtroom and from coast to coast when Jeanette Ersdale took the stand. She made a dramatic fashion statement in a short black dress and a red bolero jacket, presenting herself as a feminist picador, eager to jab the defendant with the deadly lance of her testimony. Few questions from Sachs were needed for her to get to the most damaging thrust.

"Cynthia—" she began.

"That's Cynthia Bosworth," Sachs reminded everyone. "Arnold Bosworth's wife, the murder victim."

"Right. Cynthia was in an awful state, weeping like her heart would break, when she came to my husband Elwood and me in our home for sympathy and advice the evening before that rat killed her. She confided in us she'd done everything she could to make a go of their marriage but he made her life hell. She was very reluctant to face up to the fact of Arnold's failure. She told us they were involved in terrible rows every day, every night, and she didn't feel able to keep making concessions. Elwood and I said she must divorce Arnold without delay. She said he would fight her because he loved his precious little house and refused to risk losing it in a property settlement. We advised her to go on back and tell him she was going to divorce him whether he agreed to a no-contest action or not."

"Thank you, Mrs Ersdale," Sachs said. "You have enabled us to understand what motivated the defendant to act the way he did."

"You're welcome," Jeanette said, uncrossing her long fishnet stockings. "Is that enough?"

The witness was excused.

"That's plenty," Angie said to Bobo. "I have to go."

53

While Angelica changed from tee-shirt and jeans into a more formal cotton dress, whose pale-blue and white chequered pattern prettily complemented the blue and white of her eyes, the Honorable Dr Dexter Bunn instructed the jury in the law pertaining to the case of the State of Maryland versus Arnold Bosworth. If the jurors were convinced that Bosworth, with premeditation, killed his wife, the judge said, the State was obliged to kill Bosworth—though, of course, he couched this proposition in suitably dignified euphemisms. The alleged crime and the appropriate punishment were of Old Testament simplicity: a life for a life: but a courtroom is a courtroom, with its own official language.

While Angelica brushed her long blonde hair and tied a pale-blue ribbon in it, the State began to propound its closing argument for conviction. Bernie Sachs spoke slowly and clearly enough for easy comprehension by the lowest common denominator of popular intelligence. Paul Abercrombie found his part-time friend's presentation of the alleged facts logical and deeply depressing. Paul resented Bernie's superiority. Bernie would have to beg him, absolutely *beg* him, to pay another visit. If Bernie wanted elegant hors d'oeuvres and nectar, goddamn it, he'd have to get them himself. As for cuddles….

While Angelica marched up Cornhill Street and around State Circle on her way to the Courthouse, Sachs was prosecuting faster and louder. His perorations were noted for their high emotional content, intended to incite anti-criminal indignation beyond reason. Abercrombie's subsequent plea for dismissal would inevitably seem tame, and then Sachs would be permitted to present a final argument to rebut the rebuttal. The State enjoyed an oratorical advantage.

"Where's the trial?" Angelica asked a police officer at the main entrance to the Courthouse. He directed her to the office of the Clerk of the Court, just inside the building.

"Where's the trial?" Angelica asked a grey-haired lady wearing rimless glasses, holding a telephone, at a desk near the office door. She placed a finger against her lips and indicated a chair against the wall, but Angelica remained standing. At last the telephone call ended and Angelica was awarded a grandmotherly smile.

"The toilets are at the end of the hall, dear," she said, "and take a turn to the left."

"Where's the *trial*?"

"If you mean the Bosworth trial, dear, I don't think it's suitable for little girls."

Angelica did not have time to remind the silly old fart that the trial was on television.

"My name is Angelica Bosworth," she said. "Arnold Bosworth is my father."

"Oh, you poor dear."

"I have an important message for the Defense," Angelica said. "Please tell me the way to the courtroom."

There was a guard inside the double doors to the specified room on the second floor. Angelica thrust at him a folded sheet of lined paper she had torn from a school notebook.

"Please get this to the Defense counsel," she said, managing, with a great effort, to keep calm.

The guard was a young man with a military crew-cut, who had not yet fully developed the belly of laziness.

"It isn't my job to pass children's bits of paper to counsel. They're busy in here right now. And anyway, they don't sign autographs. This ain't no pop concert."

"This is an important message for Mr Abercrombie."

"Knowing his name don't prove nothing. Anybody with a television set, anybody who's seen newspapers could know that."

"This is really urgent."

"Sorry, kid. Nothing doing. On your way."

"If you don't deliver it immediately, I'll scream and scream and say you tried to feel between my legs."

The guard was not stupid. He was quick to take the threat under advisement. Within the shortest possible time, he was down the aisle, with Angelica in close pursuit, and Paul Abercrombie, sitting beside Arnold, was reading Angelica's neatly written note. It said:

Dear Mr Abercrombie,
I am Arnold Bosworth's daughter. I have something to tell the court I know can make a big difference. Let me speak right away so it isn't too late. I promise what I have to say will help.

Angelica Bosworth

Abercrombie secretively smiled within himself. Maybe Bernie wasn't going to have everything his way, after all.

Angelica stood near the Defense table, not near enough to be embarrassed by not saying anything to Daddy. She did not have to wait long for Abercrombie's decision. His request to bring on a last-minute witness appealed to the judge's sense of theater, and Bernie did not object when the small girl climbed on to the stand and raised her hand to be sworn in.

Throughout the room there was an excited murmur of comment and speculation until it was silenced by the judge's gavel.

Angelica sat up straight and addressed the court in a voice that was girlishly high and pure, yet resolutely steady.

54

"My name is Angelica Bosworth," she proclaimed. "The defendant is my Daddy. I live in Squidgy House, our home on Cornhill Street. I am nine years old, going on ten, so I know what this situation is all about. My best friend Bobo and I are great fans of *Columbo*. We like the lawyer in *Ironside* and sometimes we even used to watch *Murder, She Wrot*e. We've learned a whole heap of stuff about crime and how it's found out. We read a lot of books."

She paused, facing the jury and looking at all of them in the front row, one by one. Some of them sympathetically smiled, encouraging her to continue.

"My Daddy is a fine man. Everyone who has read any of his books about Squidgy the Squirrel must know how deep-down *good* he is. He's the best daddy in the whole world, and I love him. A short time ago, there was a misunderstanding. I was mad at him because I thought he was unfaithful. But Betty Plowright has cleared that up. That's why I'm here to tell you he couldn't have done what he's accused of. I should have spoken before."

One of the male jurors noisily blew his nose. Many eyes were moist.

"The reason why my Daddy couldn't possibly have killed his wife, my stepmother, is because the person who killed her is me."

Arnold, shocked, jumped up, agitatedly waving his arms about and shouting, but he could not be heard. There was an immediate hullabaloo in the courtroom and throughout the fifty states and the overseas territories where the trial was being shown, live and exclusively, on UBS-TV. In the courtroom, no gavel could have quelled the tumultuous babble.

The uproar ended as abruptly as it had begun. Everyone everywhere was agog to hear whatever Angelica would say next. "I'm confessing," she said, "because I want to confess. Nobody has persuaded me to. I must, to save my Daddy from being punished for something he didn't do. I wouldn't have blamed him if he had killed his wife. He had plenty of reasons. I heard her say terrible things, threatening him and me, threatening to tear us apart from each other. She said she planned to send me away to boarding school!

"It doesn't matter what happens to me now. If he is going to be all right, so am I, even if I'm condemned to death. I don't know if Maryland executes children, and I don't care. If they killed my Daddy, I wouldn't want to live."

"Objection!" protested Bernie Sachs. "This is ridiculous."

From the spectators, there were indignant objections to the objection.

"Overruled!" said the judge with severe emphasis. There was an inviolable rule: in public, always be kind to children. He wasn't about to commit political suicide. "Let the child finish what she wishes to say," he ordered piously. "Go on, Angelica."

"Thank you, Your Honor," she said. She had impeccable manners. Many people commented afterwards on how well her name suited her, in spite of the criminal act she claimed to have committed. In court at that moment, in the bright lights of television, she looked like an angel by Botticelli on one of his better days.

Her angelic appearance, her locution, which was as innocent and melodic as birdsong and culturally high-class without being at all snooty, and her eloquence, which seemed natural and impressively mature for a girl of nine and three quarters, combined to make her an ideal popular heroine.

"There isn't any more for me to say before a proper, fair trial," she said, "except this: after I fixed the drinks to put my Daddy and stepmother to sleep, I went to the kitchen and put on rubber gloves before going to get the knife. I kept the gloves on until, everything was finished. Then I threw them away in the kitchen garbage. Police witnesses have said the only fingerprints on the knife were my Daddy's. Of course they were. I put them there. That was when I was mad at him. I'm not any more. This is the time for the real, absolutely true truth. That's all. Thanks, Your Honor. Thanks, jury."

55

Right after the judge declared a recess, Arnold summoned his defense counsel. A guard ushered Paul Abercrombie into Arnold's cell.

"It's too early to celebrate," Abercrombie said, "but I think I can detect a glimmer of light at the end of the tunnel."

"I think you think wrong," Arnold demurred.

"Your girl has certainly complicated things. But maybe we can parlay her confession into a mistrial, though frankly—"

"I'm going to make things simpler. I'm changing my plea to guilty."

"But Arnold! When I tried to talk you into pleading guilty to make a deal with the prosecution you refused. I don't know what kind of bargain we can hope for at this late stage."

"It doesn't matter. I'm going for guilty. Maybe I was wrong; maybe I really am guilty. I could have stabbed that woman after too much brandy. Or just enough. The forensic people said my blood was full of alcohol. Anyway, one thing I'm sure of: Angie could never have done what she says."

Abercrombie argued in favor of leaving things as they were, to preserve in the jurors' minds a reasonable doubt—"an unreasonable confusion. If we play our cards right, the whole case could break down."

But Arnold was obdurate.

"Guilty," he reaffirmed. "If you won't plead for me I'll plead for myself."

And so father and daughter would confront one another legally in unprecedented public conflict, each competing to be found guilty of the same murder, in order to spare the other.

Newspapers made the most of the Annapolis murder trial sensation, in the heaviest type. Baltimore's second paper produced the city's most moving headline, across six columns, on the front page:

9-YEAR-OLD ANGELICA'S SELF-SACRIFICE
REDUCES ANNAPOLIS MURDER JURY TO TEARS.

A Washington evening paper made a bid for topicality with a new angle:

WOMEN'S LEAGUE NAMES NATION'S BRAVEST GIRL:
ANGELICA, 9, OFFERS TO TAKE DAD'S MURDER RAP.

Editorial writers transcended political divisions to inspire their readers with essays of solemn moral probity and heart-rending sentiment. The most authoritative newspaper of all addressed its up-market national clientele in a homily that began:

"There are just wars that interfaith church leaders justly endorse; and there are morally justifiable homicides. A little girl of rare beauty, filial devotion and courageous fortitude has enabled us to find within ourselves a fresh awareness of the true value of The Family. Angelica Bosworth, an Annapolis fourth-grader, reminds us that any action to protect The Family is legitimate, in accordance with the highest principles, and merits our unwavering support."

Viewing figures were up in outer space, as the chief of UBS-TV put it. The public were entranced by Angelica's charm and gallant willingness to sacrifice herself for love of her Daddy.

"We're getting feed-back like no other program in the history of television," Milt Siegel exulted. "It's tremendous! All the e-mails and text messages—millions of them!—are for Angelica. The people have spoken. They don't believe in Angelica's confession—not one word of it!—but they believe in Angelica, and that's what counts."

He sighed contentedly. "You know, Ronnie," he said to his Number One Right-Hand Yes-Man, "I had a gut feeling about this story from the very beginning. I knew it would turn out this big. I have an instinct." Siegel was second to nobody in the communications industry when it came to adjusting past pronouncements to unforeseen new developments.

"Yes, chief."

56

Judge Bunn, speaking emotionally, as if in the collective voice of the nation, paid lavish tribute to Angelica's courage and dismissed her from further consideration in the case. The jury easily achieved consensus. Arnold was found guilty of first-degree homicide and duly sentenced without delay to death by lethal injection, for which he would have to wait for an indefinite time in the accommodation popularly known as Death Row. As is customary there, he was assigned a cell of his own, with a metal bed, a metal toilet and a metal mirror—everything was harmlessly unbreakable. The court proceedings were wrapped in good time for the judge's summer vacation.

UBS-TV quickly licensed Celebrity Archives Inc, to issue an edited recording of the trial telecasts on DVD, with an added commentary by Honey Laverne, highlighting Angelica's confession. The DVD was a historic, must-have smasheroo. Varoom!, almost as quickly, distributed a huge reprinting of all Arnold's Squidgy books, for which there was a clamor of extraordinary eagerness.

A couple of evenings after the end of the trial, Angelica and Bobo were at home, in the living room, attempting to play Scrabble, while Bobo's mother was busy in the kitchen. Angelica was finding it difficult to concentrate on the game, when the telephone rang.

"Please, you get it," she said, her pretty forehead corrugated by anxiety. "It's probably another reporter, and I'm definitely not in the mood for another interview. Say I'm out, and you don't know when I'll be back." She groaned. "I must get our number changed."

After a brief conversation, Bobo, with one hand covering the transmitter end of the receiver, turned to Angelica. Bobo looked excited. "It's someone called Lou Bellini of GTA," she said. "He says he has very good news."

"Ask him what."

Bobo asked him.

"He says he has to speak with you in person. I don't think he believes you aren't here. He sounds like the star of a Mafia movie, a tough guy you can't not listen to."

Angelica reluctantly took the phone.

"This is Angelica Bosworth," she admitted.

"I'm Lou Bellini of GTA."

"What's that?"

He hoarsely chuckled. Even at times of major importance, you had to keep a sense of humor.

"I'm the Creative Director and Contracts Coordinator of Global Talent Administration. You must've heard of us," he coaxed. "We're the foremost agency in the world."

"Yes?"

As was his wont, Bellini cut to the chase.

"How would you like five million dollars?" he asked. "For starters."

"Is this some kind of lottery thing? My Daddy says most of them are cons."

"I said I represent top management of GTA," Bellini pointed out with dignity. "You can ask anyone about our credentials. Everyone in showbiz, sports, communications, advertising, whatever— they all know us. Julian—Julian Grout at Varoom!—gave me your number. Your father's publisher is very enthused. Good enough?"

"I'm sorry," Angelica said, as sweetly as she could, which was very sweetly indeed. "I didn't mean to be rude."

Bellini was magnanimous.

"That's all right, darling. Everyone has to be careful what they get involved in these days. I'll tell you what I'm going to do. I'll come down first thing in the morning, so we can meet person-to-person and I can explain the whole deal, which you're going to love, I promise. OK? Don't sign anything before I get there."

"Just a minute."

"What is it?" Bobo asked.

"Maybe he's a nut case. But he knows them at Varoom! so he knows people who know Daddy."

"Well, what does he want?"

"He wants to come here tomorrow. He wants to know if I'd like five million dollars."

Bobo laughed delightedly.

"What shall I tell him?" Angelica wanted to know.

"Go for it! What've you got to lose? Let him come. He should be good for a laugh, if nothing more."

"But what do you think he wants from me?"

"Don't worry. Mom will be here. She can be your chaperone."

"And you? Will you be here all morning?"

"Are you kidding? I wouldn't not be for anything."

Angelica uncovered the receiver.

"Mr Bellini?"

"Yes, Angelica."

"Would around eleven be convenient?"

"Eleven o'clock will be perfect," he assured her. "Eleven o'clock tomorrow morning will be the beginning of your new life."

57

It was immediately apparent that Lou Bellini was a big-time operator, a high-flyer. On the upper levels of the corporate world, only the most powerful men dare look this casual. His abundant black hair curled over the ears and the nape of the neck. Obviously, he had not shaved for several days, but the stubble was neatly trimmed, probably by a costly beautician. He wore aviator shades, clumpy trainers, custom-faded, slimline blue jeans, a blue shirt with a large, open collar, and a V-neck sweater of superfine, pale-beige wool from a rare breed of llamas found only in an almost inaccessible high valley of the Andes (no, nowhere near Lake Titicaca). The sleeves, workmanlike, were retracted half-way up his hairy forearms. There was a gold strap on his left wrist, bearing a gold watch that displayed the time simultaneously on three continents and the phase of the moon and was guaranteed waterproof down to a hundred fathoms. Though he was pushing fifty years, his buoyant walk made him seem younger. He carried a slender black briefcase.

"Right on time!" he announced with a grin, when Angelica opened the door to his buzz the next morning. "I'm a great believer in getting places on time."

Angelica was slightly whelmed by his dynamic Bronx accent. She rather cautiously wished him a good morning and showed him in to the living room.

"This is Ms Simmons, my guardian, Mr Bellini, and this is Bobo Simmons, my best friend."

"Please' ta meecha."

"May I get you some coffee, Mr Bellini?" inquired Ms Simmons, vigilant minder, gracious hostess.

"Nah, I had a coffee in the train, thanks. We'll get right down to business."

They sat in armchairs in a semicircle around the silent, dark television screen, with Bellini close by Angelica.

"We have this project in urgent development the last few days," he pitched, speaking fast. "Listen to this: we're giving you *your own talk show*. It'll be the first show of its kind, anywhere, ever. Network, sixty minutes, prime time, a girl your age! Sensational!"

Angelica nervously laughed.

"Well, I don't know."

"You have the presence, the charisma, the looks, the voice. You have the smarts. You have the audience already. There are millions out there, men, women and children, who love you. They want you in their homes. They want to see you close up. Anything you say, they want to hear. All the majors are anxious to sign you up, but UBS has the logical priority, and you owe them."

He patted his briefcase.

"Have I got a deal for you! What I've negotiated only Global could get, believe me. Five million for the initial thirteen weeks, with options, plus a nice piece of the residuals and overseas syndication, plus a duplex on the Upper East Side, your Manhattan base, a company limo and chauffeur on call twenty-four hours, plus a very generous expense allowance to cover wardrobe, travel, entertainment, plus, plus, plus. It's UBS's gamble, not yours. And if the show proves the success they expect, I'll be able to bump up the terms for future segments, considerably."

Bellini smiled, then turned solemn.

"Of course in these set-ups there's always a couple of minuses as well. Global's commission is twenty per cent."

Though noncommittal, Angelica automatically did the arithmetic.

"Twenty over a hundred, two over ten, one over five—that's a million!"

"Like they say though, eighty per cent of something is better than a hundred per cent of nothing."

"So, if I agreed—"

"Agree!" Bobo blurted out.

"—if I agreed, you'd give me four million dollars."

"Spread. And naturally you'll face a tax liability, but we have the best tax accountants in the business. Anyway, the minuses will be more than covered. Think of the sponsorship potential, the endorsements, the personal appearances! A star can make a fortune on the side. You'll be an international star. The BBC's very interested and you're ideal for Japan and a whole lot of other et ceteras. Angelica, you're going to be a wealthy young lady."

"Yes, but—"

"Do it, Angie!" Bobo urged. "I'll help."

"Sure, Bobo. It's easy for you to say. But I don't know anything about television, the way it works, I mean."

"Wadya saying, you don't know?" Bellini said. "Everybody knows about television. Think Oprah! Remember Larry King! You know, their style don't you? Of course you do."

"I don't know enough about the news for a talk show, the day by day politics, the people and what they're doing."

"You don't have to. D'you think the President of the United States would know what's going on if nobody told him? Like him, you'll have a staff to keep on top of events and summarize them and put them in a few easy words to brief you. They'll do background research in depth on all your guests and even create the gags and ad libs for the autoprompt."

"I don't know how to *perform*," Angelica timidly objected.

"You did all right in the courtroom."

"That was different."

"No, it wasn't. Showbiz is showbiz. Furthermore, your producer at UBS has almost finished putting together the best back-up that money can buy, for your show, especially the best writers. Incidentally, was your confession scripted or did you wing it? Your words seemed spontaneous, fresh, sincere from the heart. If it was written, we'd like to represent the writer. UBS would pay more than he's been getting—or she. You'll have the best drama coach, the best nutritionist, the best physio, the best everything. You're already great with the public; UBS'll make you even greater.

They'll go all out with promotion. And you won't have to worry about security. They protect their own. They're not about to let some terrorist kidnap you and ruin the season. UBS has a hundred per cent security record protecting their talent."

"UBS are taking a lot for granted. I haven't said yes. I'll have to think it over."

"There isn't time for much thinking. Television is about *now*. Also, if you don't mind me getting personal, won't you need plenty of money to retain a legal dream team for your father's appeals?"

Lou Bellini opened his briefcase and took out the contract for *The Angelica Show*, in triplicate, and handed Angelica a golden pen.

She signed.

58

A distinguished Annapolitan clergyman, an enthusiastic ecumenicist who was up on current celebrity events, visited Arnold soon after he was settled in his cell.

"You must think of your present situation as a spiritual opportunity," intoned the elderly man of the cloth. "Many people on the outside would be grateful for a period of contemplation in the peace and quiet that are now yours."

He gave Arnold a paternal pat on a shoulder.

"Did you keep a diary during your trial, Arnold? I hope so. Once a writer, always a writer, eh? You could produce a valuable little book on the meaning of sin and redemption. You probably have enough time, if you get down to it without delay. You could tape an account of your experience and your philosophical conclusions, my secretary is available to transcribe it, I am willing to compose a suitable introduction, and publication would have ecclesiastical authority under my personal aegis. I'm confident there's a great readership hungering for such enlightenment. Mull over this notion as soon as you can and let me know how you feel. You can message me care of St Anne's. I'd like to stay and talk it over right away, but I am burdened by a full schedule."

He had to conduct a wedding ceremony aboard a yacht at the City Dock; and, after that, he had to have a late luncheon at the Maryland Club, in Baltimore, to console a former industrial CEO, recently bereaved by redundancy, who was considering becoming a Christian and establishing a charitable tax exemption.

The prison officers were unexpectedly friendly. Arnold learned that they and his fellow prisoners alike despised anyone found guilty of molesting a child. In fact, pedophiles in prison were in grievous danger. On the other hand, the whole prison community evinced sympathetic understanding of any man convicted of wife-killing.

"The thing is," explained Neil Houlihan, one of the more extroverted guards, "what married man hasn't ever wished his wife dead?" His hazel eyes twinkled merrily. "It's only human nature, am I right? Whether we admit it or not."

Within a couple of days of their first conversation, he revealed that he and his wife, Eileen, had been hitched for nearly fourteen years. "There's give and take," he said. "Mostly, we get along pretty good. We have to. Our beliefs make it impossible to split. And there's the kids. I have a girl, blonde like yours, who I saw when she testified on television. How old is she?"

"Angie's nine. Nearly ten."

"Angie. That's a nice name."

The thought of her brought tears to Arnold's eyes, which were pink with sleeplessness.

"My Moira's just eleven! How about that?" Houlihan marvelled that he and Arnold shared such a remarkable coincidence.

Houlihan brought in a copy of *Squidgy Invisible*, one of the early fantasies of the Squidgy oeuvre. The cover and spine of the book were worn and some of the pages foxed with age.

"Moira says this is one of her favorites," he said. "She says she's read it a million times. She wants you to autograph it for her."

Arnold was mortified to realize that in his present circumstances tears were continuously imminent. He clenched his teeth and inscribed on the title page an elaborate expression of gratitude and goodwill.

"It reminds me of an article I read in *Celebrity Confidential* about Princess Di," Houlihan said. "One of her lovers called her Squidgy. Or did the Prince call that Camilla broad Squidgy? Whatever. Is that where you got the name for your Squidgy character?"

"I had a squirrel called Squidgy, almost life-size, when I was four. Long, long before I heard of Diana and Camilla."

"It's funny how we remember our first toys, isn't it? I kept my Mickey Mouse when I was old enough to know better."

When Houlihan dropped by the next day he was eager to talk.

"Why didn't you tell me Angie's going to be a big TV star?"

"Who says?" Arnold protested. "There must've been a mistake."

Arnold was confined without the benefits of television and daily papers.

"*Newsweek*'s done a cover story," Houlihan said, waving the magazine. "'A daring new kind of talk show … Out of the mouth of babes and sucklings.' Look." He passed it through the bars of Arnold's cage. "It's in all the papers too. Didn't she tell you?"

"You know she hasn't come to see me."

Arnold felt tortured by excommunication from the person he loved most.

Why hadn't she visited him?

Why hadn't she at least sent word?

Didn't she care?

59

"Pragmatic realism, hip humanitarianism is the balance we're striving for," declared Farnsworth Stack III, like Moses distributing the tablets. The executive producer had the Angelica team gathered around the long walnut table in the senior conference room, so he could limn his vision of innovative values. The privileged young men and women at the table nodded as though in agreement, while hoping the boss might vouchsafe a few words of practical guidance.

He paused, chomping his prescription nicotine gum. "*The Angelica Show*," he proceeded, "is going to be a talk show that'll be more than talk. It'll be personality driven, of course, with focus on Angelica. But for insurance the show will be both didactic and blue-sky fun. Like Larry King's classic format, there'll be the studio desk as a secure foundation, providing authoritative continuity. Like Oprah Winfrey's iconic model, moreover, the show will sometimes move beyond the comfort of the studio sofa. The laughter and applause of the live audience is inspiring, sure, but so is mobility, surprise changes of scene. Everything will be unrehearsed, with protection only by the bleeper. I'm counting on you to think up big, relevant, tomorrow names that'll change our world, and thought-provoking travel destinations to broaden viewers' horizons and deepen their appreciation of the times in which we live. I want you to get our sponsors to put up some meaningful prizes for the competition phone-in draws, not only automobiles and two-week vacation trips. Above all, never forget you must enable Angelica to get into the heads of viewers of all ages, all IQ's and"—he allowed himself an adult witticism—"all sexes."

He quickly assumed the expression that signified "but seriously."

"Any questions?"

Nobody dared stick their neck out, so that was that.

Now the team were on their own. If the program proved to be a hit Stack would take the credit for it; if it failed the blame would be theirs.

Meanwhile, Angelica, Bobo and Ms Simmons were enjoying their duplex apartment on Park Avenue. For security reasons, the address was secret. They had palatial expanses of cream-colored wall-to-wall carpet. There were three regal bedrooms with bathrooms with golden faucets en suite, a highly mechanized gymnasium of moderate size, and a projection room of immoderate luxuriousness. The interior designer who supervised the crash job of redecoration, a lady who adored children in theory, had had the living-room bar converted into a soda fountain.

With a network personnel manager's assistance, Angelica opened an account at Chase Manhattan, in Ms Simmons's name, with two million dollars from UBS via Global on signing. It was perfectly safe to let Bobo's mother have access to the money, as she was devoted to both girls and as honest as the day is long, which, in New York in summertime, is quite long. Of course, Angelica was not old enough to write checks herself.

Everything was happening so fast at UBS that there wasn't much time for lolling about in the apartment, concocting exotic original formulas for ice-cream sundaes. There was only one hasty shopping expedition before Angelica was summoned to the studio.

The white limo took Bobo and her mother too, as Bobo, by Angelica's request, was on the payroll as companion and pop-culture consultant, and Ms Simmons went along for the ride, as official chaperone.

One of the women at Wardrobe, who was jealous of Angelica's celebrity status, was distressingly rude about the outfit Ms Simmons had selected for her charge in a big Madison Avenue department store.

"That linen thing might be all right for a DAR tea-party in Annapolis," the young assistant sneered. "This is New York."

Angelica couldn't have cared less when Bobo had told her in the store that the costume sucked, but it was for friends to give their frank opinions. Bobo, on her own initiative, discovered the assistant's name and subsequently told a junior producer about the insult.

"Thanks for letting me know," he said. "We can't have anyone sabotaging Angelica's morale. We rate morale very high at UBS. You can tell Angelica the woman's as good as fired."

There was something about being at the center of things on the inside of television that warmed the cockles of Bobo's heart. Never before had they been so warm. By means of wide-eyed girlishness and flattery, she got the junior producer to feel senior and tell her a whole passel of stuff about his importance and Angelica's place in the network.

"Mr Stack and I are really tickled we got your friend to do the show. Innovation, innovation, innovation—that's the name of the game. The media attention is terrific already, before the first night, and it's for peanuts."

Bobo snorted.

"Five million dollars is peanuts?"

"A Hollywood major name gets at least twenty million a picture these days, and points," he said. "One of our top executives got five million for his last Christmas bonus. His holiday-season bonus."

"Angelica should have got more than five million for the series?"

He good-humoredly laughed.

"She's a beginner. But, you see, we're making the show very large. I imagine someone must of slipped the Global guy a nice piece of change under the table for keeping the price down."

When Bobo, as one friend to another, teasingly confided that

Angelica was being ripped off, Angelica asked Bobo when was the last time she made eighty per cent of five million dollars.

"It's a lot," Angelica said, "even if some people get more. And anyway there's going to be more to this job than money."

"Like what?"

Angelica wouldn't say.

60

As in military planning, in theory at West Point and in the Pentagon, if not in the field, nothing at UBS-TV was left to chance. Strategic directives came down from Milt Siegel, the director of programming, for Farnsworth Stack III's tactical interpretation, and footslogging enactment by subordinates in the Scenario Wing, Wardrobe, Hairdressing and Make-Up and on the Studio Floor.

The process was not absolutely smooth. With so many top-dollar creative talents involved, there were inevitable temporary screw-ups. For example, the final, hands-on director of directors was not immediately happy with the script.

"What cockamamie kind of shit am I supposed to be working with here?" he demanded at first sight, almost choking with frustration. At his back, a ghostly muse kept asking him when he was going to compose his symphony.

His objections did not matter, being recognized as routine office politics. He always said something negative, to make sure the writers were blamed for any disappointment Upstairs when the ratings came in. In fact, the script was neither better nor worse than ever. The entries and exits and commercial breaks were designated with split-second exactitude, and it wouldn't upset anyone if there were deviations from the written dialogue. Nobody but the writers themselves would give diddly-squat.

The senior make-up artist analyzed Angelica's facial skin-tone and coloring through various lenses and his esthetically sensitive half-closed eyes, and then astonished his staff by announcing there was no need for any complementary chemical pigmentation.

"It's best she goes as is," he ruled. "Why paint the lily?" Whenever an opportunity arose, and even when one didn't, he had a way of quoting one of the few snippets at his command from the works of "the Bard of Avon," as he called him, to imbue his own work with a touch of class.

The chief designer of coiffures made her task equally easy by simply maintaining Angelica's Alice-in-Wonderland look, only highlighting, conditioning, shampooing and brushing her long, straight, golden tresses, until they seemed to glow.

Similarly, as ordered by Milt Siegel in person, the new woman in Wardrobe assigned to create the costume for Angelica's premier appearance plumped for the purity of young maidenhood. While Bobo and her mother shopped excitedly for the glamor of silk, Wardrobe prepared Angelica for the cameras by cocooning her in the milkmaid innocence of calico. Angelica was to be presented even younger than her nine years and three quarters.

After the complex razzmatazz of the advance publicity, the network played safe with the opener by giving Angelica the sort of interviewee they figured any beginner could handle.

Jessica Rose had been awarded the year's Oscar for the best performance by an actress, for her leading role in *Behold, The Dawn!* Everyone *au fait* with the way the cookies crumble in The Industry knew the award was really in celebration of the phenomenon that she was, at that moment in time, the most beautiful woman in Hollywood. Her flame-red hair, emerald eyes, ivory skin and all the rest were of beauty so mouth-watering that she had brought the most powerful studio chief to his knees. Quite a switch!

The thing about Jessica Rose that made Angelica's inaugural

broadcast register ten on the Richter scale was that the great beauty until recently had been a man. Until she revealed this fact to Angelica on air and through her to the whole developed world, nobody but a surgeon in Copenhagen had known that Jessica had been baptized Jesse.

"That's very interesting," Angelica politely commented, because, of course, she knew that talk-show hosts had to show interest in their guests. Jessica was somewhat miffed that her exclusive revelation hadn't knocked Angelica's socks off. Perhaps Angelica was too young to comprehend the enormity of abandoning a motion-picture career at the pinnacle of success.

"You wonder why I quit," Jessica said.

"You didn't like being a man?"

Jessica frowned.

"Being an actress."

"You didn't like acting, I suppose. My Daddy said he didn't think you liked it. We saw your movie."

"I'm taking this opportunity to announce I'm retiring from the screen on account of there'd be no place to go but down after best actress. Believe me, I know. There's been an avalanche of scripts and there's nothing but garbage. That's why I'm telling you my private-life secrets."

"Are you sure you want to?"

"I'm telling you for the sake of my book. I confided in a very distinguished publisher about my life-changing operations and she said doing the book this Fall will be very courageous and will have a very tremendous impact and I'll get a bigger pay-off than Harry Potter. The last Harry Potter was put out in sixty-five languages. There are twice that many countries in the United Nations. With your help today, I'll get to all of them."

"I hope it'll be worth the gamble," Angelica murmured.

"It's not a gamble. We're very confident. It's a very frank agony-and-ecstasy type book. I admit there's some very raunchy language, but it's basically very ethical. I taped everything, all my thoughts about the drugs and the escort agency years and the time I spent in Houston with the oil billionaire's widow and the post-traumatic therapy in rehab—everything's there. It's very authentic. The publisher says it's a parable for our times. It's a real page-turner. I've almost finished reading it. It's so well written I'm going to record the audio book myself. I have with me a signed copy of the proof—actually signed by me to present to you, which is very unique, the first copy, just for you. I haven't handed out any copies before now."

Angelica wondered why anyone born male would want to change (wouldn't it hurt?), so she asked, and Jessica answered at length, with genuine passion, devoting much of the time that remained between messages from their sponsors.

"Doesn't everyone in their heart of hearts wish they were a woman, if they aren't a woman already? It's a great advantage. You live longer. You control more wealth. In my case, I admit, and in other cases like mine, there is no option for biological motherhood, but motherhood by adoption opens up richer experiences. Any woman can enjoy the gratification of making trans-ethnic gestures. Josephine Baker was the outstanding pioneer role model for gathering together a rainbow international family, and many a lady of means chooses adoption today if she is too busy to set aside all the time needed for in-house gestation, with the risk of postnatal personal disfigurement. I've been considering I may pick a cute, pale-brown little girl from Polynesia. One day. Not yet."

Jessica's smile was quite fondly maternal.

"You know, Angelica, you are the kind of girl that any Madonna would be proud to take on."

Angelica blushed but kept sufficiently calm to pose the question that traditionally wraps up even innovative celebrity profiles.

"What next, Jessica? What plans?"

"Well, Angelica, here's another exclusive for your program. I've always loved butterflies. My new analyst says they are the visible incarnations of my spiritual yearnings. I have acquired a very fabulous site overlooking Topanga Canyon for a butterfly farm."

"That sounds nice."

"Yes, Angelica. It'll be a dream come true. The loveliest specimens I'm going to ship over to Venice, Italy. There's a very artistic glassworks over there where they've agreed to fabricate reproductions in stained glass and precious stones—Jessica Rose Originals for connoisseurs of jewelry for whom cost is not a consideration."

61

The popular reaction to *The Angelica Show*, as Lou Bellini of Global had predicted, was sensational. A leading national pollster reported viewer demographics across the board in numbers that broke all records for "a unique show of its kind." Most impressively, *The New York Times*, which does not eulogize television shows on its editorial page, even on the slow-news dog days, hailed Angelica's "refreshing ingenuousness, which has invested a medium sometimes criticized as jaded with born-again decency. She has reminded a vast public what it means to be American."

Milt Siegel was delighted, of course, that his judgment had been vindicated again. He sent for Angelica, and received her in his most private office, the one with the Mondrian and the terrarium containing rare cacti and a midget Gila monster. A butler in morning dress served iced cappuccino and a Pepsi.

"I want to congratulate you in person, little lady," Siegel said, beaming his first-magnitude beam. "Just like I figured, you came up with the goods. I appreciate your refreshing ingenuousness."

"My what?"

"Your style, Angelica. The other networks were getting kind of jaded. You've given the whole medium new life. When Jessica Rose volunteered for the inaugural show—she'd seen the feature in *Variety*—I knew we were on a winner. But to tell you the truth, though I was optimistic, I had no idea you'd be able to get all you got out of her. You're a great interviewer, Angelica, because you're a great listener. You let her do most of the talking. You're a natural."

"Thank you, Mr Siegel."

"*I'm* thanking *you*, Angelica. Sincerely." He examined the backs of the fingers of his left hand, as if checking his manicure for sincerity. "Now, Angelica."

"Yes, Mr Siegel?"

"I want everything to be in the open. Is everything copacetic?"

"I'm sorry, I don't know that word."

"Are you getting everything you want?"

"Yes, thank you."

"There's nothing wrong, is there? I want to know. If there's ever anything you don't feel completely happy with, say the word and I'll fix it. I want you to be absolutely, totally happy."

"Thank you."

"There's no other organization trying to woo you away from us, is there?"

Angelica merely looked puzzled.

"Never hesitate to tell. UBS is your home, Angelica. I'm going to make sure you're better off here than any place else. Would you care for another Pepsi?"

"No, thanks. There's still some in the can."

"There's plenty more where that came from," magnanimous Milt Siegel promised her.

It was sad—not very sad, but quite sad—that Pepsi Cola and all sorts of candy didn't taste as sweet when you had the money for as much, more than as much, as you wanted. Perhaps that was one of the reasons why Peter Pan didn't want to grow up.

After only a few seconds of silence, Siegel felt an uneasy twinge—not that he was suspicious or anything.

"What's on your mind, Angelica? There is something, isn't there? Lay it on the line. I can take it."

"Nothing's *wrong*, Mr Siegel. Really."

"You're a member of the UBS family, Angelica. The jewel in our crown." He had a way with metaphors, especially tried and true titles. "I want you should call me Milt."

"Thank you. I was only wondering…."

"Yes, Angelica. Name it."

"Well, there are these story conferences."

"Certainly. We have to plan ahead as much as possible. As much as being topical allows. Fortunately, your show is based mainly on human interest. Most of your programs will come out of New York, some out of LA. We can command appearances by celebrities from all over. Celebrities like Jessica Rose are dying to come to us. But we're leaving slots open for specials, the unexpected. We have one or two nice outside telecast projects pencilled in.

"That's what I've been wondering about. I haven't been invited to the meetings. Nobody tells me anything."

"There's a mass of technicalities. The meetings go on till all hours. The exec didn't want to bore you. We're sending teams ahead, to get everything set up. You'd be amazed how many arrangements have to be made—legal clearances and so on. All you'll have to do is fly in for each actual live telecast and fly right back, so you'll have used up only a couple of days."

He gave her one of his warm, confidential smiles.

"I can now reveal," he continued, "the first two almost finalized deals, and I'm sure you're going to be crazy about them. The Navy Department has given us a green light on Number One. There's this new super-carrier gone out there to the Gulf, and I'm not talking Gulf of Mexico."

He paused for a chuckle, in which Angelica was expected to join.

"The *USS Senator Charles Brocklehurst* is the biggest yet, all nuclear. Senator Brocklehurst is influential in defense circles. It'll be able to stay at sea so long, they've had to incorporate many extra new facilities to make it like everybody's hometown. There's all types of novel recreational gizmos. There's a whole college program, so sailors can qualify for genuine degrees to help them adapt if they ever opt to return to civilian life. Best of all as far as we're concerned, there's a complete, up-to-the-minute television-slash-movie studio on board, which, with satellite feed, they can hook up for live TV reunion get-togethers for crew members and next-of-kin stateside. You get the idea? That's where you'll fit in."

Another pause, a momentous one.

"They'll dress you up, Angelica, authentic Navy-style— is that cute or what?—and fly you around the ship in a chopper, for an overview. We're working on security, it's only paper-work, for you to visit the ship's own miniature nuclear submarine. That'll be a first. The other networks have never done it. And you can imagine your heart-tugging interviews with Navy-blue-and-gold kids on how they're coping with homesickness management. One positive factor is they don't feel threatened like Army and Marine Corps personnel on the ground. You'll be in a risk-free environment. Think of the visuals! We're considering giving this Navy expedition two hours' air time."

"I can imagine," she assured him. "What else?"

"The other project I specially go for is an African village makeover. This'll be a strictly green enterprise, worth beaucoup brownie points."

"What's going to happen?"

"Our location people have already found a perfect spot. A little village in Nigeria, away the hell up near an old town called Kano, that's almost on the edge of a huge desert they have up there. The village is pathetic—"

"What's its name? I'd like to find it in the atlas."

"Ngombo, Ngambo, Ngoombo—something like that. I don't have the dossier on my desk right now. It's only some huts made of mud and straw, no clinic, no school, no toilets for God's sake!, hardly anything to eat and no water within five miles, except when it rains. Perfect. We've almost finished shooting the Before footage. We're going to have to lose some of it. It'd make you throw up. We're moving some of the people out—skinny children with big bellies and eye problems and adults far gone with AIDS they haven't been taking the right medication for. Images our viewers wouldn't welcome in their living rooms."

"You can't throw people out of their homes!"

"Such broken-down-homes it'd be a pleasure to get out of, believe me. We're giving them money to go. Generous funding, I may say. And we're bringing in a photogenic bunch, suitable for the new model village we're building. We're boring for a well. The geologist says it's surprising what a little way down you have to go there. Why didn't they already have a well? Everything would've been a lot more hygienic, a lot healthier. Anyway. We're also putting in a generator. They were living without power! They'll have hotplates for indoor cooking. We may even give the village a TV set."

"They'll love that."

"No need to be sarcastic, Angelica." Siegel looked a little hurt, a little indignant. "We're going to show the world what can be done for a few hundred grand. The World Health Organisation may contribute. There are talks. There may be special one-off sponsorship from QuikSoop. Bob Geldof and Disney together couldn't make a nicer village. You'll enthuse when you get there, I guarantee. You'll find a happy community. And a lot of the credit will rub off on you. You should thank me."

"I do. I can see how we may help, if our Government does the same on a big scale. We did Africa in school. I know there are millions and millions of Africans who—"

"Absolutely! Now you've got it."

"I'll do my best."

"Good girl!"

Siegel's usual geniality having been restored, he looked pointedly at his Rolex.

"Before I go," Angelica quickly said, "please could I ask you a favor?"

"Sure. Why not? You're doing a terrific job for the network."

"Would it be all right, Mr Siegel, Milt, if I go down to Annapolis for two or three days and do a show there? I know Annapolis well. It's my home."

"Annapolis, Maryland, is where your dad's still in jail, right?"

"Yes. He's going to appeal, I think."

"If you could handle the family stress, Annapolis would be great."

"I can go then? Definitely?"

"No problem! It'll make an inspirational change of pace the week after next, when you get back from the Gulf."

62

When W. C. Fields on his deathbed was seen reading the Bible he explained that he was "looking for loopholes." Angelica's motive was different. She was riffling through the pages of the Old Testament in the hope of finding something to quote to raise the seriousness of her dialogue with Governor Simon Collingwood of Maryland, when it came to pass that she noticed a few words in Ecclesiastes that conformed with her feelings about recent events. "To everything there is a season," she read, "and a time to every purpose under the heaven … A time to kill…."

Yes, there had been a time to kill. Angelica did not regret it. Her conscience was clear, for love driveth out guilt. She regretted only that a temporary fit of jealousy had caused her to implicate her Daddy. She should have arranged the crime scene to implicate some anonymous intruder, a burglar, say, or a rival author of children's books. The trouble was that she had provided the Police Department, the State's Attorney's Office and the judge and jury with such immediately convincing clues that they had refused to accept her confession. She was not ashamed of the killing; she was ashamed of her emotional aberration. She loved her Daddy; she only hated where she had put him.

However, her confession, though unaccepted in the courtroom, had not been without benefits that continued to proliferate. It had won her her lucrative contract with UBS-TV, and sponsorship deals were pouring in like riches from some inexhaustible cornucopia.

Lou Bellini had already signed her up to endorse a variety of goods and services. So far, there were public displays of her enthusiasm for Angelica Trainers, Angelica Popsy Bars, Angelica Eau de Toilette (said to be created on a basis of jasmine, sandalwood, bergamot and ylang-ylang, in Grasse, France), Angelica Faux Pearls, Angelica Tennis Rackets, The Angelica Academy of Elocution, and even an Angelica Modeling Agency. The sky, Bellini guaranteed, was not the limit; there was no limit. These goodies, in addition to a much bigger prospective UBS-TV contract for a second series, would ensure that Angelica, if she so desired, could withdraw gracefully into prepubescent retirement by the age of 11, accompanied in luxury by Bobo and her mother. Ms Simmons was trying to persuade Angelica to call her "Mom."

With Milt Siegel's authority, Angelica telephoned Governor Collingwood's office in Annapolis and found herself connected with his public-relations spokesperson, Ms Henrietta Farquar. As in Presidential politics the Governor's campaign for re-election had begun on the day of his inauguration. Though election day was not imminent, the invitation to appear on *The Angelica Show*, already regarded as the most prestigious on network television, was an important break, for which she was taking credit.

"As you realize, Simon, the youth vote is more and more significant," she reminded the Governor over their mid-morning coffee. "When I saw Angelica Bosworth was refreshingly ingenuous, I knew I had to get her to interview you. An hour with her on UBS will be a tremendous boost to your popularity throughout the State and your status in Washington. I'm consulting again with her after lunch. I hope you approve."

"If you fix me up with *The Angelica Show*," the Governor said, there'll be a nice bonus for you."

Angelica called, as she had promised, to get Governor Collingwood's OK. Ms Farquar said she had succeeded in persuading him to do the show.

"I'll come down to Annapolis early the day after tomorrow," Angelica said, "with a full crew. I suggest we check in at the Governor's Mansion at ten for a planning session."

"A get-acquainted tête-à-tête," Ms Farquar agreed.

"I must have a private meeting with him, with him alone, off the record, before we do any filming."

"Of course. But I have to tell you it's our policy I sit on any meeting with the media and we tape it."

"Not this time," Angelica said, her voice as girlishly friendly as ever. "In fact, there won't be a 'this time' unless I get to talk with him on his own before we do the program."

"Maybe I can get him to make a special exception for you," Ms Farquar said, doing her best to seem to be an indispensable middleperson. An essential function of public relations is to seem to have a function.

"Please check and call me back right away," Angelica said, and gave her own private telephone number at the studio.

Ms Farquar, after agitatedly smoking one cigarette, called back and said she had managed to talk the Governor into making the unusual concession.

"In return for this favor," she said, "will you quid pro quo me with time in the show for the Governor to give you a quick guided tour of the highlights of our tourist attractions?"

"A deal," Angelica said, having learned some of the language of high-level negotiation. "I can promise that."

When she and her crew arrived at the Mansion, Ms Farquar greeted her like royalty. Angelica was ushered in to the Governor's parlor without delay.

Angelica had pictured Governor Collingwood with her mind's eye as an old-fashioned, avuncular figure, plumpish, with a neat white beard, like the Kentucky colonel who sells fried chicken. But the Governor looked more like the manager of an important northern bank.

"That's a fine job you're doing," he told Angelica. "It was fine that you went all the way to that crisis zone to comfort our young men who are doing such a fine job. Annapolis is a Navy town."

"Thank you, Governor Collingwood."

Without further ado, she told him what she wanted. "We'll make that Item One on the agenda," he said.

"It'll be my privilege."

He spoke as earnestly as when cutting the ribbon to declare the opening of a new shopping mall.

63

During his residence in Death Row, Arnold had soon attained monastic tranquility. He still did not believe he had killed his wife, but he was unable honestly to convince himself that the world had been improved by her living in it. He was able to look forward to his own death without apology or a sense of grievance.

Of course, his mortality was an inevitable consequence of his having been born. If he could remember the words, he thought this summer morning he would sing *Que Sera Sera*, and the thought made him smile.

"You're looking cheerful today," observed Houlihan, the friendly guard, whose eyebrows, at that moment, were raised. "Here's some mail. Word has come from the Warden that a visit has been authorized for ten-thirty, so it would be a good idea to make yourself what he calls 'presentable.' I guess that means shave yourself and comb your hair better than usual."

"I'm not expecting a visitor," Arnold said.

"I'm only the messenger," said Houlihan, handing over old-fashioned conveyances of communication, three envelopes. Letters had become rare after the first few days of incarceration. Arnold did not crave them. He did not welcome expressions of sympathy, which made him unhappy, especially when it seemed genuine.

One letter was from Naomi Swartkop of Varoom!,recommending ways he could add to the value of his estate. Why didn't he write about his recent experiences for Varoom! Senior Books—something about the philosophy of suffering? There was always a market for a celebrity's prison memoirs. If he wasn't in the mood to bare his soul in that area, she wrote, how about a valediction to his daughter? The public would lap up some intimate biographical revelations. Did he need a PC or a tape-recorder?

The second letter was from Betty Plowright. She wanted him to know how grateful she was for having known him. She asked whether there was anything she could do. There was a handwritten postscript: "Did you see the *Washington Post* report that the husband of that awful Ersdale woman is in trouble with a Senate committee investigating bribes for defense contracts? He was nominated for a Freedom Medal but now he isn't going to get one. Aren't you glad you were never involved in political corruption?"

The third letter was from Honey Laverne, requesting an exclusive recorded interview, "to leave inspiring ethical guidance to posterity."

At precisely 10.30, Houlihan slid sideways the bars of Arnold's cell to admit Angelica.

"Angie!" he exclaimed.

"Daddy!"

They hugged each other with fierce eagerness, and many adoring kisses were exchanged.

"You look wonderful!" he said. She did.

"So do you, Daddy," she replied with ardor, though he was noticeably thinner than he had been a short time ago, and there were dark bags under his eyes. "I have lots and lots to tell you, Daddy, about the tutor I'm hiring in the Fall for Bobo and me, and everything. We'll have a lovely talk later. But now I have some people with me."

Angelica, or Angie as she was at that moment, gently disengaged herself from his embrace, went briskly from the cell and brought in Governor Collingwood, while her crew, with a hand-held camera, a microphone and a portable battery of lights, set themselves up close outside the bars and switched on. She signalled to them with an upturned thumb.

"Governor Collingwood," she said, "this is my Daddy, Arnold Bosworth, the writer. Daddy, I'd like to introduce the Right Honorable Simon Collingwood, Governor of the Free State of Maryland."

"Yes, Angie." He had seen the Governor often enough on posters and in newspaper photographs and newsreels. Arnold did not understand the necessity for such elaborate identifications.

"How are you keeping, Mr Bosworth?" the Governor inquired.

"Fine, thank you, sir. How are you?"

"I'm fine."

The Governor offered his hand. They shook. The Governor's grip was hearty with practice.

"Governor Collingwood has something to tell you," Angelica said, "haven't you, Governor?" She looked to make sure the camera was running.

"Mr Bosworth," he said, "as is my gubernatorial prerogative—"

"No, no, no! Cut!" Angelica interjected. "Governor, remember we are presenting you as a human being. Sincere, plain words are best."

"Right," the Governor agreed. "Sorry."

Angelica turned again to her crew. "Governor Take Two," she said.

The Governor smiled at Arnold.

"Arnold Bosworth," the Governor said with a sudden access of solemnity that signified judicial wisdom. "I have reviewed carefully all the facts of your case, particularly the psychological implications. I have decided that for you the supreme penalty would be inappropriate. With the authority vested in me, I am pleased to inform you, Arnold, that the court's sentence of death by lethal injection is hereby commuted. So you will be transferred immediately from this place to a facility which I, as Governor of Maryland, deem more suitable."

"Governor, I don't know what to say," Arnold said.

"I wish to emphasize at this time," the Governor went on, shifting, as directed, to face the camera, "this humane commutation in no way indicates any lessening of my resolve to maintain law and order in our State, in order that our citizens can enjoy the family values they cherish."

DNA analysis of one grey hair from the Governor's head would reveal a genetic heritage from Pre-Revolutionary America and England when England was England. He was four-square in favor of supporting the standards of traditional civilization when it didn't conflict with his career.

He could have gone on speaking on the theme of his goodness, if Angelica had not interrupted the flow.

"Thank you very much, Governor," she said, "for that truly noble act of forgiveness and your inspiring message."

To her crew, she said: "OK, fellas. That does it."

64

Arnold was sitting in a softly upholstered armchair at a red-leather-topped desk in his air-conditioned suite in The Henry Kissinger Haven for the Criminally Insane. This new redemptive facility overlooking the Chesapeake Bay was a private-enterprise franchise spin-off from the State Corrective System, operated on progressive lines. Thanks to her contacts, Angelica was permitted to have Arnold's accommodation completely redecorated, refurnished and equipped to render the environment compatible with his creative persona. She organised daily deliveries by a respected up-market catering service that supplied gourmet food and drink to several major diplomatic missions in the District of Columbia.

"Governor Collingwood said it would be difficult right now to come up with a pardon," Angie had explained to her daddy. "This is a half-way house. He said it isn't as if you had to be innocent to warrant a pardon. I told him you are innocent, and he said he wasn't concerned with technical details. If you were innocent though, he said, there wouldn't be anything to pardon, would there? But that wasn't the point. He said Spiro Agnew and President Nixon were among special landmark cases. The best the Governor can offer you, when things are quiet, he said, is psychiatric reclassification and release into the community, that means back home."

Arnold had told Angie not to worry. There was no rush. He was all right.

Now he took a nibble of cold pheasant and a sip of well-chilled Bollinger, and leaned close to his faithful old electric typewriter from Cornhill Street.

"It was almost Christmas," he began. "Squidgy the Squirrel was busy counting his cache of hazelnuts...."